DARKEST
TEMPTATION

THE DARK ONES SAGA

BY

#1 *New York Times* Bestselling Author
RACHEL VAN DYKEN

Darkest Temptation
The Dark Ones Saga Book 4
by Rachel Van Dyken

Copyright © 2017 RACHEL VAN DYKEN

DARKEST TEMPTATION
Copyright © 2017 RACHEL VAN DYKEN
ISBN-13: 9781682309711
Cover Art by Jena Brignola
Formatting by Jill Sava, Love Affair With Fiction

PROLOGUE

MASON

Scotland 700 BC

*M*OTHER'S DARK BROWN *eyes crinkled at the corners. I reached up to touch the edges of her face but quickly remembered. I was too weak.*

Always too weak.

Even to catch the tear that dripped from her chin onto the threadbare blanket. I shivered as a hooded figure quickly entered the room and shut the door.

My angel.

I wanted to touch her.

My mouth burned.

My teeth ached.

She sat down next to me and pulled my head into her lap; her face was worried, pale; her green eyes flashed as she whispered to my mother, "This is the last time."

"I understand." Mother's voice cracked. "It's the only thing that keeps him strong. If my husband were to find out—"

"He would not be Alpha," the woman finished.

Alpha.

I wanted to be Alpha.

Leader.

"Born to lead." Those were the prayers whispered to me by Da.

I shivered as something pierced my neck, and then the room tilted on its side as my vision blurred into a red haze.

It could have been minutes, hours — even days — when my heavy eyes finally opened. My mother was still sitting in the same spot. Her tears were dry, her expression worried.

My arms felt stronger, lighter than they had since waking up in this cruel magical world.

"Maither?" I reached for her. "Do not scared."

"Be scared," she admonished and then pulled me into her lap, rocking me back and forth. She smelled like cinnamon and smoke.

"Tell me the story again… of the great Wolf."

She stopped rocking me as a great sadness rested against my chest like a blanket of fire.

"Oh, Mas…" She sighed. "…'tis nothing but a faerie tale."

"Please?"

She took a deep breath, and I knew it in my soul; she was about to tell me my destiny, as sure as the sun would rise and the moon soon after.

I was born to be the Great Wolf.

I closed my eyes as she spoke.

"*Those who watch were sent to the Great Mountain to watch over the humans, to keep them safe from the heavenliness, from what they could not possibly understand. They were given one job.*"

I yawned.

"*Their job was to never look away… but one day after a great battle where many children's lives were lost, one of those who Watch could not bear it anymore. He looked upon the face of one of the humans, and he fell. Because one thing you must always remember, my son. Where you look your feet will follow.*"

"*Yes, Maither.*"

"*His brethren, so distraught, had no choice but to follow, they chose to turn away from their true purpose — but not before they were warned.*"

"*I love this part.*" *I sighed and waited.*

"*Your father sang his song to The Creator, warning him that those who watch were looking away. But The Creator refused to remove freedom from any of his creation. More and more wolves sang with your father, howled their warnings to those who were falling — and yet nothing stopped them.*" *She sighed.* "*Once they fell, they were scattered throughout the human plane, given no choice but to live on earth as a prison until they are able to earn their place back in the heavenliness. They are fallen angels with black and red hair, torn wings. They are what happens when you choose yourself over your family, Mas.*"

I shivered in her arms. "*I will always choose family.*"

She nodded and kissed my forehead. "*Once they fell, The Creator wanted to reward your father. He gave him a promise that one day, his bloodline would rise up and restore what had been broken. He will be the greatest wolf this world has ever* seen. *His power unmeasurable. His abilities uncontrollable. One day he will come to restore the connection between the fallen and the heavenliness, for wolves are the only immortals who have a direct line to the stars, who know the language of the angels and freely communicate, because we are creation itself. The very earth is in our blood, our eyes. We are the purest of the immortals—"*

"*Even over vampires?*"

My mom hesitated. "*Every immortal has a created purpose. Wolves heal, we communicate with the stars. Vampires are better with their hands, able to seamlessly insert themselves in the human world and protect.*"

"*What about sirens?*"

My mom snorted. "*You'd have to ask The Creator that. Sirens are… selfish, and yet they too have a purpose, right along with demons. We all work together for the greater good, and one day, that work will all have been worth it. Because the Wolf is coming — and he will save the world as we know it.*"

Tears filled my eyes.

Hours later, when she left my room, I crawled over to the window and looked up at the stars. "*Please, please, Great Creator, let me be that wolf. I'll do anything. Let me be that wolf.*"

"*I won't hear it again!*" Father said in a hushed tone.

I crawled back to bed and hid under the blanket, but I could still discern their voices through the walls.

"*He will not be Alpha! He's weak!*"

I cringed as each word hit me in the chest like a boulder crushing bone.

"*There is a way…*" Maither whispered. "*He's stronger with their blood. It's seamless when he's bitten. If we could find a way to—*"

"You speak of heresy."

"I'm speaking of saving our son's life!" she roared. "And the only way for him to be strong is to make sure he has both bloodlines. You know it's true. We have no other children. He's the last male we've been gifted with. If not him, then who? We must take matters into our own hands!"

I stilled as the door opened a crack then closed.

I pretended to be asleep when my father kissed my forehead.

I pretended to be dreaming when he whispered quietly, "Forgive me, Mas. I've already failed you." He stood and walked back to the door. "I'll do it."

THE AIR AROUND me thickened with a sweet-smelling fog. I inhaled and closed my eyes, allowing my baser instincts to take over.

"Wolf." She whispered my name.

I sniffed. The voice was not familiar. It was not my mate. It was… other.

"Wolf," she beckoned again.

Branches crunched beneath my feet as I made my way closer to the sweet scent, closer to the warmth, closer to what I should have been running from.

I was already mated.

And yet — I was being pulled.

Like a siren's song.

I hated sirens.

Every last one of them.

But only the strongest were male.

This — I sniffed the air again as ecstasy took over — this was no male.

This was all female.

The instinct to protect kicked in, forcing a surge of adrenaline through my limbs as I staggered toward the trees.

Green eyes blinked through the fog.

I stilled.

My breath caught.

Vampire.

I frowned, reaching for her.

"Kiss me, Wolf."

Why was I tempted?

Why did I want to touch this being?

When every hair stood on end like she was foe not friend. When I had a mate back home that I loved more than life itself.

Confusion warred with disgust, and then the vampire stood on her tiptoes and pressed her cheek against mine, the way my people greeted.

But she was no wolf.

Her lips grazed the outside of my ear before she bit down onto my neck...

I jerked awake. Sweat pooled the bed like I'd just taken a shower.

And my mate, the one I was so convinced would be lying right next to me, was gone.

She'd been gone.

Over a hundred years.

And every year, like clockwork, on the anniversary of her death.

I saw my vampire.

She bit me.

And I woke up with a bruise on my neck as if it were real.

CHAPTER ONE

MASON

I SNIFFED MY way to the kitchen. There was no use going back to sleep, not with those green eyes haunting my dreams.

Nightmares.

It was always the same.

The reminder of the human I'd once shared everything with was gone, and the guilt that even during our short mating — I'd been having dreams of another — came down onto my heaping shoulders tenfold.

I was not a good man.

I was more beast than anything.

Wolves mated for life, and in my dreams I'd allowed

another female to touch me, to lick me.

I shoved the betraying thoughts away and turned on one of the kitchen lights. My eyes zeroed in on the freezer before I could stop them.

Ten steaks.

Red steaks.

Steaks with at least forty grams of protein, enough blood to saturate my mouth, coat it with its essence.

Embarrassed, I looked away.

Leave it to me to be the only wolf who craved both blood and meat. I was defective and why I'd stepped down after my mate's death.

I did not deserve to be King.

Their leader.

The wolves had each other. The pack. They had no use for me.

"Mason." Ethan, vampire pain-in-my-ass, barked out my name like he was irritated with me. He sat at the table, hands folded, black hair pulled into a stupid bun in the back of his head making him look like a female. He glared. "I can hear you."

"I know." I sniffed the air. "Where is Genesis?"

He rolled his eyes. "One day you're going to ask about my wife, and I'm going to bite you where it won't heal."

I waved him off. "I always heal. It is what I do."

"Right." His grin turned lethal.

I started turning around, but he was in front of me within seconds. Damn fast vampire pain-in-my-hairy-ass. "I'm busy."

"She's been here for two days. At least talk to her."

"No!" I barked, already feeling my hackles rise as my wolf shoved forward ready for a fight, ready to take down anyone stupid enough to stand in my way.

And then my least favorite siren in the entire universe entered the room, making the air sick with his heat. Tiny particles of dust pulsed around his body like they couldn't help themselves — damn pheromones.

He took one look at us and grinned. "You guys fighting again?"

Sirens found great joy in emotional distress, especially ones like Alex — too damn powerful for their own good. His face lit up with excitement as he glanced between us back and forth and then finally calmed the tense air, sucking it through his nostrils like my pain was his drug and Ethan's irritation his tonic.

"You done?" I gritted my teeth.

Alex shrugged. "Can't help it. I love a good fight."

"Go mate with your elf." I felt my control snapping; everyone around me reminded me of loss.

Years ago, we used to find human mates by using a lottery of sorts. We called their numbers. They mated with us. We had children. End of story.

And then the system broke.

The mates began to die.

Mine included.

And now, now that it was fixed, it just seemed like one more cruel trick of the universe that everyone would be happy; everyone would have someone but me.

Not that I needed someone, not when I had friends.

Yeah, just keep telling yourself that.

And now, now that the thirst was suddenly getting worse.

And on the anniversary of her death.

I felt — helpless. Wolves weren't supposed to be helpless; it was not in our nature.

I growled low in my throat at Alex. It only seemed to amuse the idiot more.

"Well someone should go talk to her," he finally said, "We all know I'm not allowed near humans since they tend to die from lust."

"Exaggeration," I ground out. "You didn't kill Hope."

"She's only part human." He shrugged, looking to Alex. "And since Ethan has a shitty bedside manner—"

Ethan hissed, his fangs elongating past his lower lip before he retracted him.

"As I was saying…" Alex grinned. "…that leaves you!"

"Or we can send Cassius," I offered, hating that I was even willing to send the dark angel in my stead.

Over a girl.

A simple innocent girl.

"Cassius—" The angel's booming voice shook the room. I hated it when he did that.

"—will not be going in your stead, ungrateful wolf. Go see to her injuries."

"You heard the King." Alex crossed his arms. "See to her injuries, Florence Nightingale."

"I'm a wolf not a bird." I snapped my teeth together.

Alex grinned wide. "Both are pets."

I moved to slam him against the wall, but Cassius blocked me with one of his wings; the blue feathers stood out like spikes, ready to impale me if I moved to a track.

"Fine." I jerked back. "I'll check on our prisoner."

"She's a guest," Ethan said as if I needed reminding.

I stomped down the hall and called over my shoulder. "We find all our guests in the street bloody and beaten now?"

Nobody said anything.

They didn't need to.

11

Their answers, their worry hung heavy in the air. I could taste it.

Something had happened the minute I'd touched her, the minute I'd licked her wounds.

And I would take it to my grave.

Because it was an impossibility.

She was vampire.

I was wolf.

The two did not mate.

Could never mate.

Besides, it had been my imagination.

I knew, once I set my eyes on her again, the weird longing would flee.

Anyway, I still felt the cold blood of my wife on my hands, could still feel the way she'd tug my fur.

Men rarely got second chances.

Why the hell would a wolf be given one?

CHAPTER TWO

SERENITY

I<small>T WAS TOO</small> bright.

Always too bright.

I'd been in that glaring room for two days, and each day a different immortal being too beautiful for words had waited on me hand and foot.

The angel, Cassius, had a body of stone and feathers that felt like velvet when touched. I imagined it wasn't exactly normal to randomly touch an angel's feathers, but they'd whispered when they'd seen me, as if they held secrets, as if that was their purpose, and I could have sworn the minute my fingers came into contact with them, they sighed with pleasure, shuddering beneath my touch.

Then again, I'd been attacked by a rabid wolf, so it could have been blood loss.

Blood.

I shivered as my body convulsed again in bed.

Blood. It consumed my thoughts. Made my body burn.

And then, the man with the deep brown eyes and shaggy brown hair had licked me. I'd reached for his head to push him away but had only seemed to encourage him more as I'd dug my fingers against his scalp.

And felt an energy so electric between us I wondered if I would be able to pull my hand away without dying.

He'd never visited my room alone.

The man with the haunting brown eyes.

The vampire had come after the angel; he'd looked like he couldn't quite figure me out. *Get in line, buddy.*

The siren always stayed as far away as possible; I didn't blame him.

I'd seen the aloe vera's reaction near my bedpost; the poor plant had nearly crashed to the ground in effort to lean toward the siren's smile.

I really didn't blame the plant.

He was pretty, in an inexplicable way; if you looked at each individual attribute, he was almost too pretty. But put them together, and suddenly you wondered if it was possible to keep yourself from blinking — because those seconds were seconds you had to take your eyes off perfection, and it seemed unfair, so ridiculously unfair.

The sound of heavy footsteps filled the room. I moved into a sitting position, fully expecting the angel to come crashing in.

The doorknob twisted.

And my breath hitched as the shaggy brown-haired man took one booted step into the guest room.

Completely shirtless.

In low slung jeans with more holes than fabric.

And flip-flops that had seen better days.

His wild brown hair fell just past his chin. Pieces of dark brown and orange intertwined around larger pieces of chocolate brown.

He looked like a fall drink at Starbucks.

Hot. Comforting. Yet dangerous if spilled or sipped too soon.

He was a tall dark order of pumpkin spice.

I licked my lips and forced my eyes away from his face as he slowly made his way toward the bed.

My heart picked up speed, as if it were trying to warn me we were in danger.

But the only danger I saw was embarrassment. I'd been badly attacked.

I had bruises all over my body.

And even though the bleeding had stopped a day ago, I had bites that would scar.

And I had absolutely no recollection of why I'd been walking by myself down that abandoned road in the first place.

Except that he'd been crying.

Again.

And I'd needed to find him.

I had the same nightmare every year.

And every year I searched for the source of the tears.

By stupidly walking in the dark wherever my heart led me.

CHAPTER THREE

MASON

Bᴙᴜɪsᴇs ᴍᴀʀʀᴇᴅ ʜᴇʀ cheekbones. Bite marks created tiny tracks all the way down her arms, scattering across her fingers like tiny little freckles.

The purplish tone to them told me they were healing. At least they wouldn't scar.

She was too pretty to scar.

Or at least from what I could see.

She needed to shower.

Blood still caked part of her face, and her hair was matted behind her head into a knotted ponytail that had seen better days. Nobody had been brave enough to ask her to wash herself.

The room stunk like death.

And at the same time, the sweet smell of roasted vanilla was finally starting to break through, the blood making my mouth water, and my eyes rolled to the back of my head.

It smelled like my dreams.

It felt like a nightmare.

"Bathe!" I barked in her general direction, stomping over to the adjoining bathroom and turning on the shower. I returned with a towel and chucked it on the bed then crossed my arms.

She stared at the towel and then at me. "Will you be in here the whole time?"

Her knees moved beneath the covers as she tucked them under her chin and wrapped her arms around her small body, exposing more bites. Bites that made my stomach sick.

What sort of vampire fed off its own kind?

What sort of female vampire didn't sense danger and flee?

It was a mystery. One I had no business solving. "Look, female, the sooner you bathe, the sooner you feel better and heal, the sooner you can leave."

She visibly swallowed before giving me a small nod. "Okay."

I exhaled in relief as my muscles tensed and then relaxed only to repeat the process as she slowly stood to wobbly legs and then glared at me over her shoulder. "And my name isn't female. It's Serenity."

"Of course it is... female."

Hurt flashed across her face before she jerked her head back toward the bathroom and slowly made her way across the floor.

One foot slid. The other followed.

She paused. Took a breath.

Then winced in pain as she took another step forward and stumbled.

I caught her before her face hit the ground and righted her on her feet as arms wrapped around my neck.

With a frown, I leaned forward of my own free will, ducking my nose near her neck as I inhaled my fill.

She let out a small gasp, jerking me out of my sudden mating dance.

The hell?

I would have dropped her, but she was leaning so heavily on me it would only injure her further, and as much as I wanted her gone, I wasn't a complete monster.

Carefully, I pulled her into my arms and carried her into the bathroom. I set her on the closed toilet as I plugged the drain, changing the shower to a bath.

"You will not speak." My voice sounded like nails; it was rusty, cold, angry. "You will not touch me." I filled the tub. "You will stay as still as physically possible. I will help you bathe. You will return to your bed. You will sleep."

"Please." She piped up.

I snapped my head in her direction, tilting it left then right in a predatory way. "Please?"

"You forgot please."

"I did not forget. I merely decided not to use it."

"Well..." She licked her lips. "...now's your chance, wolf."

I smirked at that. "Well-played, female. You will do all of the above... please."

She nodded. Her smile returned.

I looked away. I had no room for her smiles in my life.

The tub was filled. Now the difficult part.

A naked vampire.

I pulled on every ounce of strength I had as I very slowly peeled the shirt from her body and then tugged the soft cotton leggings from her legs.

She had no other clothing.

She was bare to me.

And I was salivating as my fangs tried to press through my gums with such agonizing want that I had to bite down on my lip to keep from biting, to keep from sniffing — everywhere.

She covered her breasts.

It made me angry. I had no idea why.

I simply knew that the lust was replaced with anger at her shame, when the human body was meant to be worshipped by wolf — sniffed, licked, satisfied beyond all measure.

My thoughts jerked me back to my mate.

Guilt intensified, stabbing me in the heart, the muscle in my chest I rarely had use for anymore.

"Get in!" It came out as demand, a bark, as anger toward her, when it was more toward myself, my own lack of control. I gulped. "Please."

Serenity stood on shaky legs, and I knew the process would repeat. She'd faceplant into the water, drown, and it would be on me.

With a calm I didn't know I possessed, I plucked her off her feet and set her gently into the water, laying her on her back as I slowly dipped her head back and ran my rough hands through her matted hair.

She closed her eyes. Her lips trembled as I tugged the knots loose and massaged shampoo into her scalp. I held her head with one hand and washed with the other. When I finished, I could actually see the true color of her hair, not pitch-black, but an autumn-brown with pieces of gold highlights that fell only near her face and at the tips. I added some conditioner Alex used for his ridiculous hair and called it good. I grabbed some soap and handed it to her.

"Do you need me to wash your soiled body as well?" I asked in a gruff voice.

Serenity looked away as her skin turned an attractive pink color. "No, but I'll need your help getting out."

I nodded and stood. "I'll stand outside the door. Just let me know when you finish."

The water was murky covering her sex.

I shouldn't have stared.

I shouldn't have searched.

I was more animal than man. I blamed my wolf side — the need to mate, to make her mine, to lick her into submission and suck her dry.

It was my wolf. He was all predator.

And she… she was prey.

It was only natural.

My thoughts must have betrayed my face. She blushed further and hurriedly started washing her body with the soap.

I quickly turned and marched out of the room and leaned my body against the closed door, finally able to breathe without tasting her scent in the air. Finally able to focus without wondering what it would be like to touch her lips, to bring her into the throes of ecstasy, to show her things only a man who contained a beast within could show her.

I gave my head a shake. Ridiculous lust-riddled thoughts driven forward by Cassius' stupid rule that each of the immortal council members had to mate for strength.

Everyone but Timber, the crazed elf-demon, and myself

remained.

It needed to stay that way.

I was strong enough on my own.

Women. Love. They did not create strength; they took it like thieves and left you weak.

And I swore I would never be weak again.

CHAPTER FOUR

SERENITY

I COULD FEEL him behind the door. I measured his breathing, counted how many times he had to inhale and exhale to get his heart rate under control.

It was my gift.

It was a curse.

Knowing how much blood pumped through his veins, knowing the exact number of times his heart slammed against his chest, crying for freedom, singing the song of his creation with each beat.

Every immortal had a song. A cadence that told vampires who they were before they even opened their mouths.

The wolfs screamed King. And yet he was in dirty flip-flops and jeans that were falling off his muscular body. His hair had a few beads in it, dirt, and I could have sworn I saw a leaf peeking through.

There was nothing about him that screamed King.

But I'd never been wrong about a song.

And his... his was different. His spoke of a legend, of love and loss. His spoke of agony that nobody should have to see in this world.

And my blood roared to life at the thought of helping heal what had been broken.

It confused me.

Wolves and vampires were not known to mate.

They weren't even really known to be anything but partners in a lifelong war against evil.

I finished washing and waited, eyeing the door to see if he would barge right back in or wait for my invitation.

The hunger in his eyes was hard to miss, just like the song of his blood. And the more time I spent with him, the more the scent of his skin — the smell of earth and life — drove me insane with need.

I cleared my throat and said only loud enough for an immortal to hear. "I'm finished."

The door cracked open.

The wolf poked his head through and sniffed.

I wondered if he realized how often he did that, sniffed the air before speaking, testing the atmosphere, analyzing.

My stomach growled.

His eyes darted to my chest and lowered. "You are hungry."

Everything he said was like a statement, as if he'd been born centuries ago and still hadn't really understood social expectations and communication. His bark, I imagined, was just about as bad as his bite — worse, since he was a healer.

I nodded my head as he took a cautious step forward and then grabbed one of the white towels and laid it on the counter. Two more steps and his warmth was pulsing all around me as he lifted me to my feet then very carefully wrapped a towel around my body. So tight, in fact, I wondered if he was worried about it dropping to the ground.

He surveyed his work as droplets of water ran down his chest. Water that had once kissed my skin seemed to glisten off his tan muscles. He gave his head a little shake as water slid to the ground near his bare feet and flip-flops.

I hid a smile by tilting my head down. I didn't want him to think I was making fun of him — but he'd just shaken his body as if he had fur, as if he was a dog in need of getting dry.

It was endearing.

Sexy.

He cleared his throat. "You need meat."

I almost choked. "Excuse me?"

"Meat. It has blood. If you eat it, you get blood. Do vampires know nothing?"

I stared up at him. "But I don't like meat."

You'd think I'd just announced that I was going to gnaw on his right arm then feed on his heart for good measure. He stumbled backward, confusion marring his face. "But… why?"

I laughed a little. "It's too gristly."

His dark, almost pitch-black, eyes widened. "Then you are eating it wrong!"

I wasn't sure why he was so offended. I tried a different tactic, sensing his anger from a mile away. His hair began to stand on end, his breathing erratic.

"Okay," I said quickly. "You're probably right."

"Probably?"

Wow, the man is impossible to get along with, isn't he? "You are right."

He exhaled, his body less rigid then before.

"I'm eating it wrong."

"You are." He apparently felt the need to comment again, and then he put his hands on his hips and let out a gruff sigh. "I'll prepare you food, and you will dress." He stopped, "Do you need help dressing?"

"I'm not exactly sure. Maybe if I sit on the bed I can manage."

He scooped me up without permission and stomped back into the room then dumped me onto the mattress.

I bounced a bit then cringed as my bruised body screamed in protest.

"Shit." It was the first time I'd heard him swear. "I'm sorry. I wasn't exactly — thinking."

Did he ever think beyond his wolf manners?

"It's fine," I said through pain-clenched teeth. "I'll be okay."

"No." He scratched behind his head and swore again. "I'll just…"

He hovered over me and then got up on the bed. He straddled my body with his. I tried not to cower in fear, but he was massive, dangerous, lethal.

He lowered his head to my neck and began to lick. And I forgot of all the reasons I was pushing him away instead of pulling him close.

I ran my hands down his bulky shoulders as the flick of his tongue moved between the bruises on my sternum; with each swipe, it felt easier and easier to breathe again, and then his tongue swirled my belly button, and my hips jerked in surprise.

He gripped them with both hands, his palms cradling them softly before digging his fingers into my thighs and moving his head between my legs.

This… this was not normal.

I wasn't injured in those places.

I hadn't been raped.

I was ready to fight him, ready to bite him if necessary and run away screaming, when his soft licks centered around each inside part of my thigh where I'd been cut years ago, where scars had marred my legs like tangled spiderwebs.

He licked harder.

And then he lifted his head just enough to look at my eyes. "Do you want the scars gone?"

What an odd question.

I frowned and then very slowly nodded my head.

"Do not bite me."

"I wasn't going to bite you," I whispered.

"You were," he snapped, and then his lips twitched into what I could only assume was his version of a smile. "It's best not to poke the bear, or in this case, bite the wolf."

"I already told you I don't like meat."

"I'm only halfway offended by that statement." He grumbled before dropping his head once again and pressing his tongue against my core.

I gripped the sheets with my hands. "What the hell are you doing?"

"Healing…" He spoke between licks. "…your…" Another swipe of his tongue. "…scars."

One last lick had me seeing an explosion of stars before he moved his head down my left leg as if he hadn't just basically given me an orgasm with his tongue.

Healing my scars, my ass.

He was taking advantage of me, using me! Using the fact that I was weak and injured to get off with his own sick wolf—

"Your anger doesn't help the healing," he whispered once he finished with the last wound on my leg. His eyes had changed from a deep dark black to a crystal blue.

I sucked in a breath. "Your eyes."

He shrugged. "What about them?"

I leaned up on my elbows, the healing all but forgotten. "They're like ice."

He jerked away so fast that I almost fell off the bed.

The door slammed behind him.

Leaving me confused, angry, and feeling used.

That was until I looked down and noticed the scars hadn't just faded; they were completely gone.

CHAPTER FIVE

MASON

I SLAMMED MY hands against the railing to the stairway. It splintered in two then fell crumpled to the ground in a heap of dust.

A slurping noise sounded behind me. With a growl, I turned. Alex sipped on his hot drink, shirtless, black leather pants tied low on his hips, barefoot, and his crazy yellow-orange hair fell past his shoulders in a heap of sunlight.

"What?" I said it slowly, purposefully showing my fangs.

He slurped more of whatever the hell was in the purple *I Heart Unicorns* mug and shrugged. "Just watching."

"Don't you have a woman to please?"

He laughed at that, "Don't want to kill her with all the pleasure, wolf. She's sleeping."

"Then go be anywhere else."

"Ethan's gonna be pissed about his stairway, all that wood." He licked his lips. "Wood, wood, wood—"

"If you won't leave, I will." I turned on my heel and stomped through the dust all the way down the stairs and into the kitchen.

Damn it, I'd promised I'd make her something to eat.

My eyes darted to the freezer as indecision washed over me. My mouth pooled with saliva.

All that meat.

All that blood.

I shook my head.

Just cook the meat, Mason. Don't eat it raw. That's not normal. None of that is normal for a wolf.

The kitchen was blessedly silent except for the sound of pots and pans hitting the stove as I rummaged through trying to find a cast iron skillet that would sear the filet mignon I'd spied earlier when I was playing mind games with myself and chomping down on the dry pinecone I still tasted on my tongue.

I jerked open the fridge, grabbed a bowl of berries, and started popping them in my mouth. Their sweet juices exploded over my tongue, coating it with sweet intensity that reminded me of tasting her. Serenity.

Hell, just my luck. She tasted like my favorite fruit.

I rolled my eyes and dropped some oil in the stove then grabbed the filet and slammed the door to the freezer only to see Cassius looming at me with a dark expression.

At least his wings were tucked back.

His arms, however, were crossed like he was pissed.

"Can I help you?" I busied myself with the steak while he paced in front of the granite breakfast bar and then pressed his hands onto the solid black rock. "What the ever-loving hell were you thinking?"

I shrugged and flipped another berry in my mouth. Raspberries, they tasted more like her than blueberries did. I made a note then burned it up in my head and ignored the pang in my chest. It matched the pain in my gut that told me I needed to eat something other than a freaking berry. "I have no idea what you're talking about. The human's hungry. I'm making her meat."

"Steak." Cassius sighed and then groaned. "It's a steak. You're cooking her a steak not making her meat."

I shrugged.

"You cooked for Genesis too," Cassius said, the air crackling with tension. "It's typical to cook for one's mate..."

I grabbed a spatula and dusted some cracked pepper onto the steak, "Genesis was a starved human who was getting fed from a psychotic vampire with a man bun."

"At least I know what you really think of me." The smell of honey and vanilla filled the room briefly as Ethan swept past Cassius and stood next to me with his arms crossed as well. "You do that to the stairway?"

I ignored him.

"The fact remains..." Cassius' voice deepened. "...you are making her a meal. After..." He cleared his throat.

"After?" Ethan perked up. "What after? What happened up there?"

"He started the mating process," Alex chimed in.

I dropped the spatula and sighed. "Does no one believe in privacy?"

"Course not." Ethan shrugged. "Just like apparently no

one believes in t-shirts around here."

Cassius looked down. "I'm fully clothed."

"Except him…" Ethan sighed. "…and myself. It's like we're the only ones who understand that clothing is necessary to fit in."

"I fit in just fine," I pointed out.

Ethan's green eyes raked over me from my worn flip-flops all the way up to my naked chest. "Sure, whatever you say, Mason. Hey, going shopping for pinecones later?"

"Bite me," I snapped.

"You taste foul," he countered. "Not at all like Genesis' sweet blood with—"

"Stop." Alex held up his hand. "Some of us want to sleep without nightmares."

"I am the nightmare," Ethan joked.

Alex gave him a slow clap while Cassius rolled his eyes. I returned my focus to the sizzle of the meat on the stove. If I focused on solitary things, then I didn't think about Serenity — the way she tasted, the way her body had responded to mine so perfectly, so effortlessly.

Damn it. I was such a fool.

I'd loved once.

I'd mated once.

And now I was alone.

I scratched the back of my head and turned off the stove, not realizing that the room had fallen silent behind me.

I quickly turned.

All three men were staring at me as if I'd just announced I was going to sprout wings.

"What?"

Alex's eyes went black as he stood near Ethan, as if he was protecting him, which was insane. Ethan could hold his own against any of us. Cassius' wings sprouted from his back, the tiny feathers completely erect, ready to shoot like arrows into my naked chest. His eyes were white, his skin marble.

"Guys?" I sensed no danger. But I did sense fear. From everyone but Cassius.

His head tilted, and he sniffed the air, his eyes rolling to the back of his head before his eyes returned normal.

The air froze as Stephanie, Cassius' mate and the last remaining Dark One, made her way into the kitchen. She arched her brows and whistled. "Freaky, Mason. Seriously freaky."

Alex gave his head a shake then slowly returned to normal while Ethan's eyes searched mine.

"Would someone please tell me what's going on?"

"Lie to me, and I impale you," Cassius said in a threatening voice.

Good to know I was still on his good side.

"How many years?"

"How many years?" I repeated dumbly.

"How many years…" He approached slowly. "…have you craved the blood?"

I sucked in a breath as shame washed over me. Shame that I had hidden it from the only family I had ever known.

Shame that it was a secret I'd kept my entire existence.

"Since my first hunt," I admitted in a grief-filled voice before I slapped the steak onto a plate, grabbed utensils, and fled the room.

CHAPTER SIX

SERENITY

My body was still buzzing from the contact of his mouth. My heart felt like it was cracking, and I had no idea why. What I did know?

I needed some sort of blood if I was going to get my energy up. Normally, I had my small apartment stocked in emergencies.

Well, this was an emergency.

A bird chirped outside my window.

I shuddered. Gross.

The idea of killing a tiny innocent bird made me want to puke. I was officially the worst vampire in existence. I couldn't even kill right. In fact, I'd never killed before. Most of my kind at least enjoyed the hunt, but I hated it. I hated the fear I saw in creatures' eyes.

Besides, it was not like we needed to hunt. It was more of a hobby for people now that modern technology made it easy for us to take blood however we needed it.

We survived off blood and food — both helped nourish. Where food kept our bodies running, blood kept us young and viciously strong. It was like taking a drug that promised perfect vision, hearing, and all of the above.

The vampires that had died out were the ones that had wanted a real life with humans. There wasn't a timetable of death for our kind; we were immortal. But the problem with introducing humans as mates?

It caused vampires to want to die.

Why exist outside of the family you helped create?

My own parents were no longer alive, choosing to die together rather than live another hundred years.

They had left me enough money to live comfortably.

But part of me felt... angry.

And a huge part of me believed I hadn't been enough for them to stay, that my love for my parents wasn't even a flicker of the love they had held for each other.

I hated the whole immortal code.

The mating process meant you weren't yourself anymore but part of something bigger. I didn't understand how people could say the mating was so great and wonderful when it made you forget about your own child.

Or abandon them.

It had been my job to plan their funeral. They'd made a big deal about it. Mom had gotten dressed up. Dad had worn a tux.

And I'd had to sit there and watch them wither away. I had even offered my veins, butthey'd politely declined. And then they were gone.

Dust.

I swallowed past the lump in my throat as a vision of them holding hands fell to the forefront of my mind. The smile on their lips...The way they'd died together looking at one another...

Rather than at me.

Their only daughter.

I shivered and shoved open the window.

It wasn't good blood. But it would do.

I locked eyes with the bird and beckoned it. "*Come.*"

It flew to the windowsill and looked up at me. It was pretty with golden-flecked eyes and tiny little feet.

I choked back a sob.

What if it has a family? What if I am taking it from its parents? What kind of monster am I?

"Be free, little bird." I shoved it away.

See? Worst vampire ever created.

"You let it go," a gruff voice said behind me.

Clearly, I lacked blood if a wolf could sneak up on me. I was in a pitiful state; maybe I should die too.

Like my parents.

What else did I have to live for?

Nothing.

I was all alone in the world in a job I hated and apparently a target for no reason other than I was probably going crazy.

Stupid dreams.

I shrugged. "I wasn't hungry."

His look said he didn't believe me, and when my gaze fell to the steak, I almost jerked the plate out of his hands and bit into it without using the fork.

"Told you." He smirked knowingly. "Sit down, and I'll cut it up."

He was true to his word. The big bad scary wolf literally cut up the steak into tiny bite-sized pieces as if I didn't have a mouth full of fangs ready to punish the meat into submission.

He finished then stabbed the fork into the meat and held it out to me. "Small bites. Don't rush it. I don't want you getting sick."

So now he cared?

With a shaky hand, I took the fork and then shoved the meat into my mouth. I groaned and closed my eyes. When I opened them, he was watching me with such intensity I felt embarrassed. "Sorry, it's been a while."

"Since you've eaten?"

"Since I've had good meat," I admitted. "Nobody knows how to cook it right. I went vegan years ago."

"A shame." He licked his lips as his body seemed to grow before my eyes. Maybe it was because he was sitting so close to me, but something about him looked different, altered, and very other-worldly. I hadn't met many werewolves; all the races typically kept to themselves.

The immortal council made sure that fights were at a minimum.

And since I was literally in their main house under their protection, I could only assume that this wolf was *the* Wolf, the one who kept the packs in line.

Demons, wolves, vampires, angels — it was a gas, our fun little immortal world.

Word on the street had been that the demons were somehow finding their souls. That there was an elf goddess who'd set them free.

It seemed like a bunch of crap until I'd seen a blue-eyed demon at a bar last week who'd actually waved at me and then kissed a human right on the mouth without killing her.

I was so lost in my thoughts that I didn't realize I'd finished the entire steak.

I patted my stomach. "Thank you. I was starving."

"Your stomach was loud. Believe me, the entire house was aware of your pathetic state. Vampires need food just as much as they need blood. Meat helps repair red blood cells and keeps your body running at its best. Pair that with your daily doses of blood, and you should be good to leave by the end of the week."

I gulped.

I want to leave, right?

Why did the idea of going away make my chest ache?

He took the plate from my hands and stood. "I'll be back to check on you. Go sleep."

And that was it. The door clicked shut behind me. The bird returned to my window, and I was left wondering if I would always be in this state.

Alone.

Wishing for more than I had.

And cursing myself for wondering if it would have been an awful thing had they just left me to die.

CHAPTER SEVEN

MASON

I CLEANED THE dish, wiping it with a rag at least a dozen times before placing it back in the cupboard. I wasn't sure how many minutes I'd stared out into the empty space of the kitchen.

Until a ripple of awareness ran from my hands all the way down to my bare feet. The spells always happened this way, as if I was possessed by some sort of monster inside that needed to be fed — demanded it.

"Drink," it whispered.

I clenched my teeth and braced the counter with my hands as claws started sprouting from my fingers, digging into the hard granite like it was dust.

Normally, I could control the urge.

I always had.

Not this time.

This time, I felt the blood coat my tongue, the taste of ecstasy as it built in my body.

"Cease." A booming voice came like a clap.

My claws retreated, and I looked up into the face of Cassius.

With a sigh he tilted his head. "You cannot fight it forever."

"I can." I snapped my teeth together. "I'm just weak because of her."

"Then continue the mating process. You and I both know you already started the minute you decided to heal her a second time. Every time you lick her, the link between you intensifies. This is not a fire you can control. It's a blaze that will sear you alive."

"No." I ignored the need to charge up the stairs and love her, mate her, make her understand that this predatory thing between us was more than just healing. I was lying to myself if I believed otherwise. I chose the lie.

He sighed. "Stubborn wolf, you will mate with her. You will stop ignoring your destiny."

"My destiny has already passed," I whispered with emotion. "It died the minute she did."

"She…" He leaned in until we were face to face, until I could feel the ancient secrets his wings whispered into the air. "…was not your destiny."

With that, he walked off leaving me pissed and confused and near starving.

I reached for more berries and snarled in disgust as Ethan

waltzed in with a bag of blood and a cruel smile on his lips. "We're leaving for a few days."

"We?" I repeated. "You and Genesis? The twins?"

"We, as in the council. Each of us is going back to our respective… roots to warn the different immortals of what's to come. The war has just started. We have fallen angels all over the place trying to decide which side they want to fight for, and the most evil of all has returned to the abyss to play house. I'd say it was time to warn them, wouldn't you?"

I couldn't argue that logic.

"The wolves, they will also need to know…" Ethan's voice trailed off.

"Let Cassius tell them."

"I imagine they'd prefer you," Ethan said softly.

The pity in his eyes wasn't helping.

Nor the hollow ache in my gut when I thought about my pack, my people, the looks on their faces when I'd walked away and sworn never to return.

My shame was too great.

The burden insurmountable.

"Three nights." Ethan was talking again. "Think you can keep the house from burning down?"

"I'll make an effort." I tried joking, but it fell flat on my own ears. I was trying too hard to pretend I wasn't aching. Always aching.

"That's really all I can ask." Ethan winked and then, just like he had appeared with Cassius…

They were gone.

Utterly alone.

Solitude used to be my peace, my… serenity.

I jolted away from the counter as gasps fell from my mouth. Serenity. It was gone. My comfort in my loneliness

was gone.
  Replaced with…
  Her.

CHAPTER EIGHT

MASON

I PACED IN the living room, my bare feet creaking across the hardwood floor. Every few minutes I'd look up at the ceiling and wonder if she was sleeping, if she was suffering.

One more lick.

I could heal her completely.

It would cost me everything to make her well.

And I had never been in the business of licking a vampire whose idea of foreplay included sucking on my arteries.

My body jerked to attention.

Damn it.

I was wolf.

And yet the idea of her lips pressed against my pulse, the feel of my teeth digging into her flesh had such a dizzying effect on my equilibrium I tripped over the carpet and nearly faceplanted against the black leather couch.

Vampires.

I was halfway between paranoia and blood lust; at least that was what it felt like, this crazed need to run up the stairs and do something unthinkable.

What the hell makes any of my family think I am able to control myself without someone watching my every move?

Maybe that was part of their plan.

Nobody was here to stop me.

Nobody but me.

Hell, I'd be better off chained in the basement.

My thoughts perked up. Now, that was actually a solid idea born out of necessity to keep my body, my tongue, my mouth from the one woman who would take it all — and refuse to give it back.

I'd be lost to myself.

She'd be lost to me.

And I didn't know how to be an *us* anymore — maybe I never had. I'd been a horrible mate to begin with. What sort of mate dreamed about other women? I'd loved my human mate.

But she had been frail.

I'd been in a constant state of fear whenever we joined, fear that I would kill her with a flick of my wrist because I wasn't cautious enough.

It would be difficult to injure a vampire.

I shook the thought when a knock sounded at the door. My ears strained to hear what was on the other side.

Heartbeat.

Rapid.

Even breathing.

I sniffed the air and then rolled my eyes as I stomped over to the door and jerked it open.

Timber grinned at me with white teeth and creepy blue eyes. "Just checking up on my old friend."

I almost slammed the door in his face. "We have never been friends."

He took a step over the threshold and spread his arms wide. "Fine. Cassius said that you were going to lose your mind and either kill a vampire or screw one. Had to see so for myself."

"Hate demons," I muttered under my breath as I made my way back to the living room to my pacing, to my torture.

Timber spread his massive body out on the couch and let out a pleased sigh. "Is she pretty?" He sniffed the air. "She smells pretty."

My hand was on his throat before I could stop myself, squeezing with the intention of a good kill — blood — though demon blood tasted like ass. I wondered if Timber's would be any different since he'd been saved by Alex's mate, the last remaining elf and only immortal able to give life back to the damned.

I felt my fangs elongate as my mouth filled with saliva.

Dark hair fell across Timber's sculpted face as confusion replaced his smile. "Have you looked in a mirror recently?"

"Why do people keep commenting on my body?" I growled, releasing his throat and closing my hand into a tight fist as my talons shoved back into my fingertips like they hadn't just been clawing out and itching to rip flesh.

Timber didn't even rub his neck. He merely examined me again like I was a complicated puzzle that needed solving.

"At the risk of getting choked again—" His eyebrows shot up. "—you're... other."

"Other?" I repeated. "What the hell does that mean?"

Without warning, he lashed out with one hand and slammed me across the face so hard all I saw was blood; all I wanted was his death.

He jerked away and jumped behind the couch laughing. "Well, well, well, now I know why Cassius wanted me to check on you. You're a ticking time bomb, aren't you?"

"I'm not a bomb. I'm a wolf." I pointed out the obvious, hoping to deflect more questions that I didn't know how to answer. Like why I could hear the whoosh of blood in his body as it pumped from his heart to his extremities, and why, if I looked close enough, I could hear the whisperings of the blood as it communicated with the rest of the body.

Timber stopped walking and turned, looking over his shoulder. "You should feed before it becomes impossible to control."

I rolled my eyes. "Got that covered. Had enough berries to make a fat bear happy, and I'm hunting later."

"Hunting?" This seemed to perk him up. "You do realize it's illegal to hunt humans?"

"Humans?" I laughed. "I'm hunting for pinecones."

He pressed a hand to his forehead as if I was giving him a headache. "Pinecones." He nodded. "Yeah, let me know how that works out for you. And remember what I said. You need to feed." He tapped the side of his neck. "Preferably not on me when I piss you off again."

"You wish," I spat.

He winked. "You have the jaws of a kitty cat, wolf. I imagine it would tickle."

I moved to him.

He stumbled back and then gave his head a shake.

Go away, I said mentally. *Just. Go.*

He shook his head again and then narrowed his gaze on me. "Careful with those thoughts, Wolf."

I blinked in confusion. "My thoughts?"

"This is going to be a shit storm," he mumbled more to himself than to me. "Feed, mate, and join the ranks in helping us fight Those Who Watch." He pointed a finger at me. "In that order."

"The Ones Who Watch are behaving…" I sighed. "… for now."

Timber groaned. "You know nothing, Wolf! We have ten of the ancient fallen angels running around a modern-day society with all of its… temptations… and you think the problem will lessen? You do realize that the Originals stood on a mountain for years simply watching life happen rather than participating in it? And you think that they're just going to listen to us even though we freed them? That they'll give up the power they have here?" He spread his arms wide. "Look around you! They would be considered gods!"

"Blasphemy," I spat. "Immortals were placed here to protect humans from that very thought. The council—"

"Exactly," Timber agreed. "The council is out fighting a war we can't win unless we stick together. Hell, I have Alex's wife out with me restoring demons' souls in alleyways! All of this, while you stare at your pathetic little pinecones and focus on all the things that have gone wrong in your life and all the reasons for your inability to actually live. You know?" He clenched his teeth. "You want to die so bad? You feel so bad about yourself? Ask Cassius to end you. Better yet, ask the One to take your soul. You're a shell of a wolf, a shell of a man, and not worth another wasted breath." He flipped me off and slammed the door behind him.

I stood there, stunned.

Shame came swiftly.

Because the demon was right.

I'd helped save Alex. I'd helped save Hope after Alex begged me, but only because she was a friend. The mindless humans milling around the world had no idea what was coming, and frankly I didn't care.

Because I was hurting.

Because I was afraid of myself.

Afraid to even look in the damn mirror and see the signs that everyone else had been seeing for the past two days.

I shook with the memory of her bloody body.

And when my tongue touched the blood in an effort to heal, a booming voice screamed in my head.

"Awaken."

Maybe the monster wasn't outside the house. Maybe I was the monster.

Maybe I was the one they should fear.

CHAPTER NINE

SERENITY

I WAS EITHER losing my mind, or Mason was outside howling at the moon. In a tangle of sheets, I finally got out of bed and walked over to the window. He was standing in the same worn jeans as before, only this time he was completely barefoot as the moon cast a silver glow over his face.

It was as if he was growing before my very eyes. I was no wolf expert, but even I knew that they stayed the same size throughout their immortal lives. Wolves didn't grow with age.

And yet he was definitely increasing in girth.

This morning he'd been at least two inches shorter than

when he brought me his steak. His biceps, while impressive before, now stretched and strained against his skin as if they were dying to break through. The night air blew his hair across his sharp cheekbones.

Every inch of skin was just barely containing an arsenal of muscle that was so impressive it was hard to look away.

I gulped out a "Wow."

Mason's head jerked up to the window.

I completely froze.

His dark eyes locked on mine, and then very slowly lightened to an ice-blue. Another wolf trick I'd never seen before, not that I hung out in their packs.

He started walking back toward the house. I could feel my heart in my throat as his heavy footsteps gave way up the stairs and finally down the hall until the door to my room was shoved open, and he ducked inside.

His shaggy hair was kissing his shoulders as he made his way toward me slowly, cautiously, as if I was the danger, not him. Muscle stretched across his abdomen and stomach, glistening with a sheen of sweat.

I gulped and then whispered, "I didn't mean to interrupt whatever you were doing. I just… I heard you."

He frowned. "Heard me?"

I felt so stupid. "Howling."

He cracked a smile. "It's not called howling. It's called singing."

I squinted up at him. "But… it sounds like a howl."

He smiled a bit more, making me feel warm inside instead of afraid, lonely.

"To a vampire, it sounds like a howl, a protective intimidation technique. It sounds the same to humans. But to the angels? The stars? Or our own packs? It sounds like…"

He looked lost in a dream as his face broke out into a smile. "…it sounds like the song of salvation."

"Is it always the same?"

"Always." He shrugged. "The howl, as you call it, was passed down to the immortal wolves, a gift from our creator, a way to create protection over our packs and young while giving him the glory for it in the first place. It is our cry to return to the stars, our thanks. It's the story of our beginning and the eventual story of our end." He looked down, his eyes closing. "It has been a long time since my song has joined others."

I reached out, thought twice about it, then just soldiered forward and pressed a hand to his arm then squeezed. "Why?"

He looked down at my hand, confusion marring his brow before he placed a hand on top of mine and then very slowly ran his thumb across my skin.

I shivered.

"I am their leader, but I found I couldn't lead the way I needed to when my mate died. I left my second in command. It is better that way."

I closed my eyes and listened as his blood roared to life beneath my touch almost as if it was attempting to escape his body and join with mine. I'd never felt another person's blood call so strong, like an invisible tether beneath the skin just waiting to latch on.

As the silence stretched, I was able to focus more and more.

The blood started to chant *"King, King, King"* like before.

He stopped brushing his thumb over my skin.

I opened my eyes just as one last chant fell from the blood. "Yours."

He removed his hand and pulled away, his eyes searching mine with intensity I hadn't been prepared for.

"What did you hear, vampire?"

"King," I said honestly. "Your blood says King."

He jerked his head away; his eyes focused in on the moon again as if it would help him with the heaviness that he carried with him like a battle scar. "What else?"

"What makes you think there's more?" I asked cautiously.

He gulped. "Nothing." He shook his head. "It's... nothing. You should sleep. I'll check on you later—"

"Wait!"

He turned on his heel. "Yes?"

"Can I maybe... go downstairs and watch a movie or something? I'm going a little stir-crazy up here?" I knew it was a long shot. The guy liked to be alone, and apparently, howling at the moon was his favorite pastime.

I waited.

He eyed me up and down then bit firmly on his bottom lip before tucking his hair behind his ears in obvious irritation. "Fine."

It was more of a bark than an actual word, but I was taking what I could get when it came to him, and I was desperate to leave my bed. Besides, I had an entire season of *Outlander* to watch.

I'd just been getting started on the last season when I'd fallen asleep and then somehow been attacked as I'd been searching for the man who'd called to me.

I shivered and followed Mason out of the room, slowly measuring each step as a wince of pain rocked through me with each movement.

I would do anything for blood.

Blood would fix this.

Blood would make me feel better.

I felt my vision blur just as Mason's strong arms wrapped around me. Why hadn't they at least offered blood? Ethan was one of the oldest vampires in the world; he had to know I needed blood.

Why hadn't any of that occurred to me before?

Mason grunted and placed me on a soft leather couch then pointed to a blanket. "Genesis calls it a throw. I don't know why the hell a blanket of fur is called a throw, but regardless, if you get cold, you can use it."

I wanted to remind him that vampires rarely got cold when another tremor wracked my body, reminding me yet again that my vampire side hadn't been itself ever since Mason had licked me.

"Is Ethan here?" I asked in a small voice.

He full-on glared. "Why would you need Ethan? He's mated."

"What does that have to do with anything?" I said in annoyance. "I just figured since he's a vampire, he'd know my ne—"

I stopped short when Mason pounced in front of me and grabbed my chin between his fingers. "Needs? You think he can measure your needs? Am I doing such a horrible job?"

"You're angry," I whispered, tears filling my eyes. "Why are you angry?"

His nostrils flared. "Am I not doing a good enough job for you? What else could you possibly need? I fed you. I gave you a blanket. I made you comfortable, and I healed your scars!" Each word came out louder than the next until his body was humming with barely pent-up aggression.

I instinctually tried to pull away.

He just held onto me tighter.

"What. Do. You. Need?" he repeated.

"B-blood." I felt shame. I didn't know why. Maybe it was because I felt weak, and I hated it; maybe another part of me didn't want to seem dependent. But it was a way of life, and it was what helped give me life.

He dropped my chin immediately and staggered backward. You'd have thought I'd just told him the boogey man existed and was living in my head.

"Mason?"

He shook his head and then bit back a curse so loud that my ears rang before he stomped away, and from the sounds of it, was breaking things in the kitchen.

Tears overflowed my eyes until I heard him coming back. I quickly wiped my cheeks and tossed the blanket over my body, not only so I looked like I was comfortable, but also to put a barrier between us.

Like a fur blanket would do anything if he wanted to pounce. I was a weak little lamb compared to his bear-like stature.

"Here." He thrust a glass in my direction, causing some of the contents to slip over the edge and onto his hand.

Blood.

He looked down, his breathing heavy. "Take it, damn it!"

I grabbed the glass before it spilled, noticing how his hand shook as blood dripped down his fingertips. His eyes flashed blue again, and then he was bracing himself against the mantle on the fireplace. I was afraid he was going to break it in half.

"Drink," he urged in a gravelly voice that didn't sound at all like him. It sounded more beast than man.

I chugged the blood, gulp after gulp; its tang was like thick tonic to my soul as it healed me from the inside out, knitting things back together that had been broken and numbing the pain that had been debilitating for two days.

I carefully put the glass on the table. "I'm done."

He exhaled and turned; his blue eyes locked on to mine. "How did it taste?" His voice was still animalistic by nature, his eyes crazed. If I hadn't known better, I'd have thought he was… Aroused… which should have terrified me; instead, I felt hot all over as his gaze raked up and down the blanket as if he could view me beneath, see my skin.

"Good." The word finally tumbled from my blood-stained lips. "It tasted good. Thank you."

He inclined his head and eyed the glass.

Did he want it?

I frowned at him.

He shook his head and then grabbed the remote and tossed it on the couch. "Go wild." He started to walk off.

"Wait!" Why was I calling the monster back into the room again? "Um, where is everybody?"

He stiffened. "The council is out on official business for a few days. It's just you and me."

I couldn't help the gulp, just like he probably couldn't help the look of pain that flashed across his face as he glanced at me and the glass again.

"So, stay and watch *Outlander*?" I offered.

"Out what er?" he repeated, "Is that a movie?"

I gasped in outrage. "It's only the best show on TV!"

"*American Ninja Warrior* is the best show on TV," he argued. "Damn Ethan, won't even let me try out."

I covered my mouth with my hand to keep the laughter in. "You would either kill the contestants or be too heavy for the obstacles."

His head whipped in my direction. "Did you just call

me fat?"

My eyebrows shot up. "The only fat part of your body is probably your head."

"Thank you." Sarcasm was apparently lost on him as he took the compliment and then let out a little half-bark-half-laugh. "You called me a fathead." His smile grew. "Vampires, so mature…"

"Hey, you're the one running around throwing temper tantrums and breaking things then getting angry at me one minute and—" I gulped as his eyes flashed then locked onto mine.

Shit.

"I'm not angry at you," he finally said, looking away.

"Then who are you angry at?"

"Everything else." He took a seat far away from me and nodded to the television. "Show me this *Outlander*. I'll decide what's better."

"And if it's better?"

A smirk replaced his scowl. "If it's better, then you win, and I cook you steak again. If it's not better, I win, and you go hunting with me."

"Deal." I held out my hand.

He stared at it for at least three seconds before grabbing it, dwarfed by the size of his hand, and giving it a shake. He didn't let go; instead, he tugged me closer to him until I almost splayed across his lap and then touched his nose to my neck and inhaled.

He rubbed his head against mine and spoke softly in my ear. "This is how wolves make bets."

I gulped and whispered hoarsely, "Noted."

CHAPTER TEN

MASON

I NUZZLED HER neck.

I was a freak.

She smelled — healed.

My nose touched her chin as my mouth watered with the need to pierce flesh.

I jerked back and gave my head a shake, my hair whipping against my cheeks so hard I probably looked half crazed.

Her eyes locked on my mouth.

I licked my lips instinctively.

Expression dazed, she blinked up at me and then frowned. "You smell... different."

"Now I smell?" I lightly shoved her away from me. "You're not the best at compliments, vampire." I nodded toward the TV. "Let's get this over with. I have a hunt to take you on."

Her eyes narrowed in on mine before she directed her attention to the set and pressed a button on the remote. "Game on." She scooted away from me.

I felt the distance in my soul. As if she'd just put this invisible barrier between our bodies. I sucked in a sharp breath to ease the pain, to help myself calm down.

But my blood boiled beneath the surface of my skin.

It demanded I pay attention.

And just as the screen changed to music, I knew only too well that music reminded me of so many years ago when I was born. I fell into a familiar trance...

"Take him!" my mother screamed. "Take him from me!"

"We will be killed for this," Father whispered hoarsely. "Nobody must know, not even Sarial."

"He sees all!" Maither wept over my body.

Blood. Why was there so much blood?

Flashes of light burned my eyes.

"It was the only way, mo leannan."

With a cry, she threw herself over my small body, "He will be stronger than us. He will be stronger than them all."

The light burst through my eyes. What had just been darkness turned to a bright shining sun as heat enveloped my body. I lunged for my mother.

My father held me back.

I was two.

I saw blood red.

I felt their pulses.

I felt their hearts.

I wanted to rip them out with my teeth.

"Son!" Father held onto me so tight my lungs burned. "You must control the lust."

I screamed. I fought him.

I just wanted.

"Son, if you do not control yourself, you will kill everyone you love. You will destroy your life before it even begins. You must learn self-control."

I understood the words.

Werewolves talked at one year old.

At two, we were expected to hunt.

I gave my head a shake.

A thundering sound pounded my ears, and I covered them with my hands and screamed as the archangel Sarial swept into the tent.

He eyed both of my parents.

And finally me.

"He is no longer your son." Sarial's eyes went white. "He is other. If he stays, he will kill you." He jerked his attention to me. "What do you hear?"

"B-blood!" I raged.

He pressed a hand to my forehead. "And now?"

"Sleepy." I yawned.

He picked me up into his arms and gave my parents one last look. "Your punishment for what you have done. You will stay in this state until he makes his choice."

"My baby!" Maither wailed. "Give him back!"

"Silence!" Sarial waved his hands, and immediately no words came from her still-moving mouth. "You know the cost of creating."

"He is ours." Dad stood to his full height. "We made a pact to—"

"I know exactly what you have done!" Sarial roared. "You

have taken matters into your own hands because you lack trust. Therefore, I will take what is most important to you before you suffer the consequences of his blood."

I didn't understand.

I didn't want to.

What did they do to me?

I felt normal.

Except for the burning in my lungs… the parched feeling in my mouth…

As Sarial carried me away, I saw my tears fill my mother's eyes. All I kept thinking was that I would never see them again. I would never know love again.

My mom ran after Sarial and handed him a pouch.

Inside were berries and pinecones.

"We will meet again." Dad nodded to me. "Be well, son."

My vision faltered.

It was my last memory of my parents.

Of Scotland.

Of the large castle and the grounds around it where vampires and immortals lived and protected one another.

I gasped for air just as the music stopped, and the show started to play before my eyes.

It was painful to see the scenery. I could almost smell the heather.

I looked away. "Turn it off."

Serenity frowned. "But it just started—"

"I said turn it off!" I jumped to my feet and kicked the coffee table over; the glass fell to the ground with a shatter as tiny droplets of blood spread themselves wide over the hardwood.

I sucked in a heavy breath as Serenity froze next to me.

I could have sworn the world tilted on its axis as I eyed

the three drops, not even enough to make a mess; one swipe of a cloth would cause them to disappear.

Weak.

I was so weak.

I rocked back on my heels just as Serenity stood. "I'll clean up."

My wolf howled with outrage.

That was what I called it.

Because I refused to believe that there was something else lurking inside my body, begging to break free.

I was bad.

A monster.

My own mate had told me I was too heavy to lie on her after I'd licked her dry, after I'd pleasured her.

If someone who loved me was afraid of me, of the way I looked in the steamy throes of sex, of the way my fangs pointed differently than others of my kind, of the way I asked if I could bite her — begged her even...

Then where did that leave Serenity?

A stranger.

Where did that leave me and my place in the world?

I punished myself well for my monsters.

I just never realized there would come a day when they wouldn't recede, when they wouldn't listen — when I suddenly wouldn't care if they broke free and destroyed me and everyone else around me.

The longer I stayed in that spot...

Staring at that blood...

The longer I thirsted beyond all reason.

And the longer I wanted to lick the blood dry then turn my attention three inches down Serenity's neck where her pulse sang.

"Mason..." My name fell like a whisper from her lips. "...calm down."

"Never—" I clenched my hands into fists as claws started breaking through my skin. "—tell a wolf to calm down when he is angry."

She pressed a hand to my shoulder.

I didn't jerk away. My body instantly calmed. I frowned down at the blood. "How did you do that?"

"Do what?"

"Make it go away?"

"I don't understand?" She moved her hand.

The rage returned.

Adrenaline pumped through my system.

Run. I need to run.

Before I could think any more about the blood, about her touch, about what any of it meant, I turned on my heel and ran out of the house.

Through the trees.

Picking up speed.

Until my wolf broke free.

Until I shedded my human skin like one would a Halloween costume and morphed into a wolf that was the size of a small Honda.

I knew what people saw when they viewed my transformation. A black wolf with dark eyes and huge teeth.

I made my way to the river and leaned over to drink my fill.

Only, when I saw my own reflection, I did a doubletake.

My fur.

It was not black.

It was blood red.

My eyes black.

And as if seeing a stranger for the first time, my wolf-self smiled with a secret.

Dread threatened to overtake me.

I was not in control of myself.

I tried to stop smiling.

I told myself to look away.

I lost.

CHAPTER
ELEVEN

SERENITY

I DIDN'T THINK anything of it when Mason didn't return right away.

But after five hours, I started to get worried.

It didn't help that it was getting dark, and I was in a strange house all by myself. A house where I wasn't sure I could stay hidden and or protected from whatever had tried to kill me the other night.

The more I thought about it the more I pulled the blanket closer to my body, tempted to throw it over my head as if it could make me invisible.

The clock struck ten, nearly sending me off the couch in

a fit of fear. I was a vampire, for crying out loud.

I could hold my own.

I just didn't want to have to.

And I wasn't exactly in the best practice to do anything outside of throwing a few punches and running. Besides, I'd had one cup of blood that was quickly leaving my system.

"Stop being ridiculous," I said to myself literally as the doorbell rang and then the door opened.

I froze as the scent of burnt wood invaded my nostrils only to be replaced by what smelled like campfires and summers spent on the lake.

"Mason," the deep voice called, and then I was staring into the deepest blue eyes I'd ever seen in my entire life and trying not to panic over the fact that the strange man looked like a successful male model with a lucrative underwear campaign. "Oh, hello." He smiled.

I frowned.

He looked away and grinned as if he knew the effect he had on people and then tried again with the smiling at me. "I'm Timber. And you are?"

"Serenity," I said, lamely staring at his outstretched hand.

With a sigh, he left it there just hanging between us.

I had no choice but to shake it.

His grip was firm.

I decided I liked him even if I didn't want to; it was impossible not to at least be mildly intrigued by his pretty face and apparent good manners.

"Have you seen the wolf today?"

"No…" I took my hand back. "…but I saw the man about five hours ago."

He choked out a laugh. "Same thing. I was hoping he would be here so I could discuss—" He turned. "Never mind. Seems the wolf is home."

Mason staggered into the living room looking like he'd just gotten in a fight with a semi-truck and lost.

Blood caked his fingernails.

And his sandy brown hair suddenly looked like it had been dipped in red.

"What the hell happened to you?" Timber let out a whistle.

Mason growled, and then his piercing gaze was on me. "I'm—" His eyes rotated into the back of his head.

Timber reach out and caught him just before his forehead slammed into the wall.

"Mason!" I ran over to his body and examined the cuts and bruises lining his arms before Timber laid him across the floor and pulled out his phone.

"Something's wrong!" He barked into the phone. "Do I look like a veterinarian?"

He rolled his eyes while I cupped Mason's head in my hands. His perfect lips parted just enough for me to see fangs.

Werewolves typically had shorter fangs than vampires; it made it easy for them to tear into meat without them getting in the way.

They didn't, however, have fangs that elongated past their lower lips.

That wasn't right at all.

"What do you mean you have a feeling?" Timber roared. "I'm not going to base this off a feeling!"

I ran my fingers over Mason's strong face. Something was horribly wrong.

A garbled moan came from his mouth.

I leaned closer, pressing my ear to his chest. I just wanted to make sure his heart was beating, that he was okay. I had no idea why I was so worried about a stranger. Maybe because of the way he'd taken care of me? Maybe because his blood still sang for me.

Only this time, it sounded like it was in agony.

"I'm not so sure that's a good idea," Timber whispered into his phone. "I'll keep her away just in case."

I turned my head to Timber. "Just in case what?"

He hung up the phone and then paled.

Just as teeth pierced my neck.

CHAPTER TWELVE

MASON

"*Yours,*" Her blood sang.

"*Mine,*" I said right back.

I was crazed, angry, hurt. I was so many things.

And then she pressed an ear to my chest, and my heart thumped with purpose, with new reason.

And instinct completely took over.

An instinct to claim.

An instinct born into me from hundreds of years of trying to do exactly the opposite.

I burned for her in a way that made no sense.

I pined as if I'd been searching for her my entire life.

My body begged.

My heart thundered, demanding I give answers I couldn't give to questions I refused to ask myself for fear of what I would discover.

And.

I.

Snapped.

"Mason!" Timber was yelling. "You're killing her!"

Her eyes rolled into the back of her head.

Why was Timber angry?

Why was she dying?

No, no, this couldn't be wrong.

Not when it felt so right.

So good.

I felt her everywhere.

In my blood, in my mouth, coating my fangs.

More. I wanted more.

To strip her bare.

To expose every inch of her to my mouth.

"Let. Her. Go." Cassius' voice shook me from my state.

Why was Cassius suddenly there? What was wrong?

I'd never experienced such pain as I released her neck and fell to the ground, Serenity falling across me, a bloody mess.

I'd done that.

I'd put that empty dazed look in her eyes.

Oh God, I'd hurt her.

I hurt everyone.

I scrambled backward, my head knocking against the wall as I tried to swipe the blood off me, but there was so much, and I still wanted it.

I wanted all of it.

Wasteful.

What the hell was wrong with me?

Serenity finally came out of her paralyzed state. When she looked at me, it wasn't a look filled with fear.

It was a look filled with disgust.

I disgusted her.

I disgusted myself.

This was why I'd been taken from my parents.

Why I'd stopped being King.

An abomination.

A fool.

"I'm—" Damn it. I couldn't even get the words out; my voice sounded all wrong — gruff, loud — like it wasn't me speaking at all. "I don't understand."

Cassius let out a long heavy sigh that shook the room with its force before his wings pointed down and then disappeared behind his back. "Timber, take Serenity upstairs—"

"No!" I roared, as if I had a reason to keep her by my side, protecting her, harming her, nearly ending her life. "She's…" Stunned, I tried to erase the word from my mind, from my very existence.

"Mate. Mate. Mate," my blood chanted.

Hell, I could hear her heart begin to pound; mine raced right along with her. I'd just somehow sealed our fates. I should have known all along it would be my lack of control that would do it.

I should have known.

I closed my eyes. "Go."

"Mason—" She opened her eyes.

"Just go."

I felt her disappointment in the air like a crackle of sadness splitting us in two, separating our hearts when all they ever wanted were to be next to each other.

I was losing my damn mind.

Once Timber and Serenity were gone, Cassius took one look at me and scowled. "You need to be more careful next time."

"Tell me I heard you wrong." I snorted. "There will be no next time. It was a mistake. I just... I've been having weird—" I gulped. "—weird cravings."

Cassius sniffed the air. "Half lie. More omission than anything. Alright, I'll bite." He grinned at his own joke.

I just covered my face with my hands and prayed he'd kill me and get it over with.

"How long have you been having these... cravings?"

"Why do you always ask questions you already freaking know the answers to!" I roared.

His eyebrows shot up. "Alex's yelling, I'm used to. This is new for someone normally so calm, so reserved, so loyal." He made the word sound dirty.

I glared and then flipped him off.

The bastard laughed even harder. "I can't wait to tell Ethan."

"You aren't telling anyone." I stood to my feet, wobbly, but at least I was standing. "This is a onetime slipup, a mistake a—"

"Why do you think her blood sings to you, Mason?"

I ignored the burning truth in my chest, the signs, the monster within. "Because I'm a wolf. I stopped eating red meat. Red meat contains blood. Therefore, it's a misplaced craving." There. That sounded good even to me.

"You are not what you think you are." Cassius' eyes went white as a chill overtook the room. Great. Just great. I hated when he went full-angel. Especially now that I'd tasted blood, now that I'd messed up so royally I was most likely going to get struck down or at least punished. "And yet, you're exactly what you think you are. You're just too scared to admit it."

I looked away. I had to. The truth was like a punch to the chest.

Blood, mine and hers, covered the floor.

Mine, from trying to claw my way from the war with my wolf, the one where I'd tried to throw myself from a cliff in an effort to take back control.

And hers, from my attack.

God, I'd attacked her like the monster I was.

Like a savage animal.

I still tasted her on my lips.

"Hmm…" Cassius tapped his temple. "…our pasts can only stay locked up for so long. Don't you ever wonder why your human mate died to begin with?" His wings spread out from his body like tentacles testing the air. "You mated with one because it was how things were done, but your soul has always belonged… to another."

He disappeared.

Without judgement.

Without punishment.

And maybe that was the point. I'd already spent an eternity in a prison of my own making. It would be useless to give me another.

When I was so good at staying in mine.

Until now.

I eyed the stairway with hesitancy.

The stairs creaked under Timber's weight. "I feel like I should stay and watch the show, take notes, make popcorn," he teased, "but if what Cassius just whispered in the air is true, then I probably don't want to be anywhere near this house for another few weeks."

"Out." I jabbed my fingers toward the door.

He grinned and then shrugged. "Maybe if you stopped keeping secrets from your friends and family, you wouldn't lash out and bite the first girl who wants to adopt a puppy."

"I will rip your throat from your neck with ease, demon. Now leave."

He leaned in. "After what I saw, I think I believe you. Have fun!"

He shoved past me.

The door slammed.

One heart beat.

I counted its rhythm; I told my heart to match it.

And the strangest thing happened.

It did.

CHAPTER THIRTEEN

SERENITY

My neck burned.

Blood caked my fingertips.

I wasn't healing as fast as I normally did, and that thought alone shot every last nerve I had.

I could feel his teeth.

He hadn't even numbed me.

Just tore right in like a complete animal.

It was the most terrified I'd ever been in my entire life.

And then.

Pleasure.

So much pleasure.

His. I felt his arousal through the blood; I felt the rightness of what he was doing even though he was doing it wrong. He was a messy savage with no restraint.

And I loved it more than I should.

My heart had soared for his, even as he'd drained my body.

My only thought had been, *"Take your fill."*

Even if it meant my death.

I'd been so disgusted with myself I could barely look at him before Timber took me from the room.

The fact that he'd been able to even send me away after tasting for the first time, after experiencing the link between our minds, the crashing rightness I felt between our souls…

Was a terrifying thought.

If he pushed me away, if he left me, my future, that psychotic wolf with bad manners and chef-like tendencies, I wasn't sure my heart would survive.

It was already too fragile from my parents.

I heard his heart speed up — mine matched it — and then his scent was everywhere, different from before, sweeter, as if he'd just rolled around in honey and forgotten to shower. Then the spice was back filling the air with more flavor as I tried to calm my breathing.

The door opened.

He'd changed into new clothes and wiped most of the blood from his body.

His eyes were crystal blue.

His feet bare.

His low-slung jeans made a noise as they rode low on his hips and pressed against his tan skin while he crossed the room.

I licked my lips and finally gained enough courage to

speak. "So… you, uh… still hungry?"

"It's not funny." He ran a hand through his shaggy hair and cursed.

I lifted a shoulder, "It's sort of funny. Who knew wolves could bite like that?"

He exhaled and bit down on his lower lip so hard it turned white, and then his eyes were on my neck darting back and forth with uncertainty. "Let me heal you."

"It's nothing." I covered the place with my hand where he'd bitten me and came back with more blood staining my fingertips. "I've survived worse."

"I doubt it." He leaned forward, his massive body hovering over me. "Please, Serenity, let me fix this."

His plea hung heavy between us.

There would be no fixing what had been done.

I leaned forward and pulled my hair over my left shoulder, bravely exposing my gaping wound to his lust-crazed eyes.

Bad idea?

Maybe.

But I stupidly trusted him.

Maybe it was the link between us; maybe I was just as sucker for deep brown eyes that flickered to blue and pierced the air with sensuality unmatched by anyone I'd ever met.

Mason leaned forward, his face inches from mine.

Maybe that was what had gotten me in this predicament in the first place, my inability to separate the fact that he was both beast and man — and I was easy prey.

His tongue very tentatively reached out and slid across the skin near my collarbone and then higher and higher, and with a moan, he swept over the wound. I felt my skin knit together, fuse from his healing abilities, and when the pain finally subsided, he rested his head on my shoulder.

I ran my fingers through his hair while he picked up my free hand and licked a cut I hadn't realized I had.

His tongue felt smooth against my skin. I immediately wanted it in my mouth, pressed against every inch of my body — even the parts that didn't need healing.

With a shudder, I pulled my hand away.

He lifted his head, eyes so blue they reminded me of ice.

I saw the truth in his eyes. I saw the sentence he didn't want to utter. I wasn't sure if I should be offended, hurt, both? I bit down on my lip, took a gulp of air into my lungs, and whispered, "We're mates."

I figured if I said it aloud, it would sound less terrifying.

It wasn't.

He was a council member.

An immortal king.

I was a part-time college student with no purpose and no friends outside of school and the small coffeeshop I frequented where Mike, my barista, added extra espresso into my mochas with a side of blood.

I kept people at arm's length.

Because I was afraid that if they got close, the truth would slap me in the face.

I wouldn't be enough to make them stay.

"I had a mate," Mason whispered, "before."

"What happened to her?" Jealousy flared to life over this nameless, faceless woman who'd shared his heart like mine — who'd kissed his lips and touched his skin. I wanted to rip her face off.

Mason tensed next to me. "It would be easier to tell you the story if you stopped thinking of all the graphic ways you could dismember her."

I gasped. "Werewolves don't read minds."

"Not typically…" He sighed. "…no."

"How?"

"That's not the story you asked for, and it's not one I know how to tell." He gave his head a shake. "She was frail. I always imagined I'd be mated to a warrior, someone who understood my needs, who allowed me to take care of them. And she did all those things — but I always felt fear from her. It made her love feel tainted. It made me feel like I wasn't doing enough to keep her happy, to keep her safe." His voice cracked. "We had just found out she was with child when I woke up to find her dead next to me, no explanation, no reasoning. We'd been together so long we'd wrongly assumed that we were safe, that she was safe."

I gasped and covered my mouth with a shaking hand. "I'm so sorry."

"So am I," Mason whispered. "So am I." He moved and stood in front of me, his blue eyes locking onto me with such intensity I was afraid to breathe. "When balance was restored, and Ethan married Genesis, a war broke out, a war we cannot fight unless we're at our strongest."

I was afraid of where this was going. "My parents said something was coming. They just never said what. They didn't involve themselves with immortal gossip. They thought they were above it."

"Gossip?" Mason ground out. "And why do you talk about them like they no longer—" His eyes searched, found the answer on my face, and then looked away. "I'm sorry too. It's a hollow feeling, one that is never quite filled again."

I nodded. "So, what now?"

He looked hesitant and then almost embarrassed.

"Mason?"

"I, uh…" He jerked away from me so fast the moment

shattered. He ran a hand through his shaggy hair and then eyed the door as if it were a narrow escape route he may not make in time. "…I should." He gave his head a shake, his eyes going from brown to blue then back again.

"Mason?" When I said his name a second time his eyes stayed a blazing blue. I held my hand out to him. "Mason, are you okay?"

He went completely still. "Don't speak."

I gave him a small nod as he closed his eyes and looked like he tried to breathe with great effort. I didn't want to be afraid, but if he attacked me again, there would be no way to fight it, no way to fight him off whatever.

"Can't." He shuddered. "I can't anymore."

I stood.

He held out his hand to stop me; it shook as his fingers snapped and twisted, revealing a giant claw that could rip me in half if I breathed wrong.

"Mason, listen to my voice." I was basically worthless as a vampire. I was fast, but not fast enough to escape him, and not strong enough to overthrow him.

Weak.

Is that why they left?

Why everyone leaves?

"Ever since you came…" His chest heaved. "…I have no control." His teeth snapped together as the muscles in his neck flexed like they were seconds from snapping. "Just stay the hell away from me!" he roared.

He jerked the door open, and it went flying behind him, slamming against the wall nearest the bathroom.

I took cover as a piece of wood flung in my direction and hit me in the elbow.

When I lowered my arms…

Mason was gone.

CHAPTER FOURTEEN

MASON

I PULLED AT my hair over and over again as I walked around outside the house in mindless circles. The craving had lessened in her arms. Licking her had been…

My everything.

And just like that, when the hunger for her had died down enough for me to think, a small voice whispered, *"Take."*

I put up a mental block against that voice.

And lost my shit all over the place when it pushed back; the hunger burned, my temper snapping.

And I broke a freaking door.

I lived by my control.

I fed the regulator like a well-tended pet with a schedule. I'd always been in charge of my urges, sexual and otherwise.

I kicked a boulder, sending it sailing into a tree, cracking the poor oak in half as it fell against the road.

Well, shit.

I stomped over and shoved the tree out of the way as if it was a feather. I was getting physically stronger, sharper, hearing things I had no business hearing.

Like the music of her blood.

Her heart calling to me.

I fell to my knees.

The desire to bite her was just as powerful as the desire to mate with her, to take her from behind. My hands shook as I dug my claws into the earth and braced my body in a hunting position.

The more blood I was exposed to the worst it got.

And I could feel her blood mating with mine, swirling around in a dance so ancient that even I didn't know all of the movements. But my blood did — hers did. It recognized its mate and was rejoicing while simultaneously pumping to all the wrong areas in preparation for the final joining.

I scowled as my heart thumped in my chest.

If I never completed the mating, it wouldn't matter. She was immortal; she would survive it.

I, however, wasn't sure I would.

And that is the problem, isn't it?

What if she was weak like my last mate?

What if she hated me? What if I killed her?

So many what-ifs and so many scenarios I didn't understand how to fix or control.

I would not risk her.

I would not.

"You sure pout a lot for a male." Cassius suddenly appeared next to me.

"Didn't hear you," I grumbled, still in my protective positioning.

He shrugged and looked back at the house. "I brought reinforcements."

"Everyone's back?"

"Alex thought it would be best for Hope to discuss war strategy with Timber. They'll be back later this evening."

I groaned. "You didn't have to cut your trip short. The fight between good and evil is more important than my… cravings." I gulped.

Cassius' eyebrows shot up. "What makes you think your cravings aren't a part of that war, Wolf?"

Frowning, I looked down at the same earth I'd sworn to protect, its minerals swirling beneath the surface, kissing my fingertips. I belonged in the dirt, outside; I belonged with what I'd sworn to protect, and yet, I'd abandoned it. "This war is better off without me. I'm not that important, Cassius. It took one weak human to prove that I am nothing. I can't fix what's been broken."

"Maybe you can…" Cassius hesitated. "…maybe you can't. But the point…" He tilted his head and then leaned down next to me, his feathers shaking as pieces of dirt flew up and touched them, changing their color from blue to brown and back again. "…is to try."

The dirt fell back to the ground in an array of colors and burst into a small field of wildflowers where my fingers were pressed. "Angels and their tricks."

He shot me a half grin. "You know I don't control the wings. Sometimes I think it's Sarial's way of still speaking to us, always creating, always moving." He locked eyes with me. "I do not control them. I'm a part of them, and they are a part of me. Control does not always equal good. Sometimes, control is evil."

"Control keeps things in line."

"No..." Cassius turned and started walking away. "... control is just another word for fear."

I watched his body disappear through the woods and glanced back down at the wildflowers, finally deciding on picking them as I wiped my dirt-covered hands on my jeans, and made my way slowly back to the house.

Serenity was downstairs with Genesis, her smile genuine as the girls huddled over a magazine.

Ethan's green eyes narrowed in on me as he sniffed the air, and then his eyes widened a bit before he elbowed Cassius.

Cassius just shrugged. "Let it go."

"This isn't frozen," Ethan said through clenched teeth. "This is going to be a clusterfu—"

Genesis cleared her throat and held out one of the twins to Ethan. He sighed and took both of them out of the room, but not before giving Genesis a disgusting kiss on the lips and shooting me another threatening glare.

"He slobbers all over you," I pointed out. "You can't enjoy that."

"Twins." Stephanie swept into the room. "I'd say she enjoys it very much."

I made a face and lamely dropped the wildflowers in front of Serenity. "For you."

I inwardly rolled my eyes at myself. *Is that the best I can do?* I may as well have brought in my latest kill with its tongue hanging out and panted next to her like a new pup.

Serenity held the flowers to her nose. "Thank you."

"Thank Cassius." *Why did I say that? Why am I speaking still?* "His feathers created them with their creepy angel magic."

Serenity's face fell. "Oh." She laid the flowers back down on the table like the gift wasn't really a gift anymore.

"You're the one who picked them." Cassius brushed a kiss across Stephanie's nose.

Happy couples. Everywhere.

Disgusting.

Even an angel had a mate.

I snapped my teeth in irritation and jerked open the fridge door in search of something to eat.

"Alex, damn it!" I slammed the door closed. "Did he take all the food?" My berries were gone. Not a pinecone in sight. There was nothing in the damn fridge but ketchup and a glass jar of pickles.

I opened the freezer. I knew I had stored some frozen berries in there a while back.

Nothing but meat.

And a frozen pouch of blood.

I swallowed.

The room fell silent.

I slammed the fridge shut, opened it, and slammed it shut again, throwing an unbelievable tantrum that I couldn't control even if I'd wanted.

"Looks like you need to go to the store," Cassius said calmly. "Take Serenity."

I held my laugh in.

It wasn't funny.

He wanted me to take a vampire that I wanted to devour alone, in a car, to a store that had every single piece of meat my wolf would kill to buy, to eat, right in the damn aisle.

"I love grocery shopping!" Serenity jumped out of her chair.

I gave Cassis a middle finger and then did it again just for good measure.

"When my parents were alive—" She stopped talking and looked down at the ground.

Hell.

I was screwed.

Her heart raced.

And then her jumbled thoughts pumped out. *"Not enough for them to stay."*

My heart cracked in my chest as the words tumbled out of my mouth. "I'll take the Jeep."

"You can make a list while he drives." Genesis winked at me.

Stop being helpful.

Genesis was one of my best friends. But she also had a gold medal in manipulating me into doing things I didn't want to do, like during Christmas when Ethan wouldn't watch Hallmark, and she'd said she'd comb my fur if I sat next to her.

I loathed to admit the times I'd choked up watching those damn movies.

Within minutes, I was driving Alex's new shiny white Jeep Wrangler through the downtown traffic in search of Whole Foods while Serenity sat stock-still next to me.

I'd been forced to put on a shirt and nice jeans with a pair of flip-flops that I reserved for outings. But when I'd come downstairs, Genesis had sent me back up to shower the dirt from my hands and face.

I was a wolf. Wolves were meant to be dirty.

The argument hadn't stood.

So, I'd pulled my hair back into a rubber band, put on the too-tight white t-shirt that made my chest itch, and managed to get in jeans that I assumed would split in two if I bent over one too many times.

The minute Serenity had seen me, her heart raced a rhythm that made my blood soar.

She wanted.

I wanted back.

And we were alone.

Mating in the back of Alex's Jeep actually cheered me more than I thought, but it was wrong.

All wrong.

Wolves and vampires did not mate.

Someone got something wrong.

And if I lost it all…

Lost her…

Lost anyone…

Control, control! I ripped the wheel and cleared my throat as I turned into a parking spot near the front of the store. "So, you like grocery shopping?"

I inwardly groaned. Was I always this bad at decent conversations with people I wanted to lick?

Maybe that was the problem; I'd never wanted to lick anyone, claim anyone as badly as I did her. It made me stupid.

Sex made everyone stupid.

But at this point, I'd probably get first prize.

Serenity grabbed a cart and smiled up at me. "Yeah, it was one-on-one time with my parents. We'd always grab a Starbucks and then run around and find all the best bargains on food. We never ate the same thing every week. My mom liked keeping things fresh and exciting. Some weeks we did pasta one day and a casserole the next, since we don't really eat to survive." She shrugged. "We eat more for pleasure than anything else."

I swayed when she said *pleasure.*

My eyes swam with lust.

She steadied me with her hand on my arm.

"Sorry," I croaked then looked down at her hand and took it in mine, helping her push the cart toward the produce section.

I didn't want to let go.

I knew I should.

It would be the wise thing to do.

Because I was minutes away from stripping her naked next to a head of lettuce. That damn well would cause a need for clean-up on aisle four.

"Relax..." she whispered. "...it's just grocery shopping and a little hand-holding. It's not marriage. You don't have to keep me." Her heart stuttered a bit.

I felt her pain, the intense need to be needed. Wanted.

"It would be more than marriage." I spoke in a quiet voice, releasing her hand in order to grab the same lettuce I was hell-bent on pushing her up against. Carrots. I mindlessly started tossing things in the cart without any sort of purpose to keep my hands occupied. They wanted her skin so bad I couldn't focus. My teeth kept pressing against my inside cheek, imagining piercing her soft flesh.

I gripped the cart again.

Serenity seemed to know the storm that brewed inside as she very gently kept rubbing her thumb over my hand.

"It's scary. This whole mating business."

A fresh wave of guilt hit me. "I wish it wasn't me."

She stopped walking.

A horrified expression had me picking her up into my arms and holding her against my chest. "Get that thought out of your head. It's not you... I'm just..." I swallowed the lump in my throat. "...I'm a broken, dirty mess, and you don't deserve the mess. You deserve the masterpiece."

Tears filled her eyes as she reached for my face then slowly cupped my cheek. "Mason, the mess is the masterpiece."

And then, very gently, she pressed her lips to mine in a chaste kiss that had my lungs burning for more, my body hard and aching.

"I wish..." My eyes searched hers. "...I wish I believed you."

"Me too." She gave me a sad look as she slid down my body.

I felt her breasts against my chest; I wanted to grab them, see them fit into my massive hands, watch her scream my name. I wanted so much.

I didn't know how to have her — without losing control.

Without giving in to whatever the hell was wrong with me.

"I don't want to hurt you again," I admitted in front of a box of Cheerios.

She grabbed the cereal and tossed it into the cart. "Have you ever thought that maybe if you drank more blood you'd be able to think clearly?"

I frowned. "But wolves don't drink blood."

"Right, but you're... not... just a wolf." She said it with slight hesitation.

"Are you suddenly a vet?" I joked and grabbed ten more boxes of cereal. Genesis loved cereal, and Hope, it seemed, was either pregnant or Alex needed to feed her more. She constantly ate at midnight, giant bowls, sometimes three.

"I could be wrong." She eyed some oatmeal and tossed it in the cart. "If I'm wrong, I'll go hunting with you."

My ears perked up. "Do you think you can keep up?"

She smacked me in the chest.

It only stung a bit.

I rubbed the spot and winked.

She was so pretty, my mate.

Hell.

I needed to stop thinking that way before I screw us both, making it so she couldn't escape me, escape the bond.

But she was pretty.

So pretty.

Her eyes flickered green.

"Hungry?" I asked.

"Starving," she admitted. "I would probably eat two of your steaks."

I groaned at the erotic picture. "Wolves like to make food for…" I didn't say *mates*, but that was what it was. It was our job to hunt the food, prepare it, provide for their every need.

I frowned at the memory of my last mate not liking steak but eating it because I'd wanted her to.

Then frowned harder.

"You alright?" Serenity asked, steering the cart into the meat aisle,

"Yeah, I'm just—" My mouth went completely dry.

"Stunned into silence over meat?"

She crossed her arms while I stared, while I lusted, while I briefly imagined becoming a butcher and licking the table after I prepared the food.

And then Serenity, in all her beauty, reached for some steak, sniffed it, then held it out. "This one's good."

I'd never been so wrongly aroused in my entire existence

as she licked her lips, held the steak out to me, and provided the only two things I needed in life in one shiny package.

Her.

Steak.

Her.

Steak.

I felt my body give way. I tried to control the urge, but I was too late. I opened my mouth to say something, probably *run*, but before the word could get out, she grabbed my hand and jerked me into a door that was for employees only. She tore at her own arm then held it to my mouth.

I took her blood.

My wolf roared to life as I pressed her up against the wall, my teeth locking onto her wrist, my body pinning her next to the employee-of-the-month chart, my damn eyes glued on Bart, the winner of February, and then the chart fell to the floor as Serenity rubbed her body against mine.

The friction in my jeans was too much.

She reached down and flicked open the button.

And then my mouth was on hers.

Hers on mine.

This. This is what I should have done yesterday.

This.

She gripped my length as I rubbed instinctively against her, devouring every cry she made as if it was the sole purpose I'd been put on this earth.

Not here.

We couldn't. She was better than that.

But I couldn't stop.

I was going to have to call Ethan from prison.

And explain that I mounted my mate in the employee break room of Whole Foods — and liked it.

"Mason..." She purred my name as I cupped one of her perfect breasts in my hands. It was heavy and formed perfectly for my palm. It was mine.

I dug beneath her shirt, desperate for more, just as she reared back and sank her teeth into my neck.

My wolf roared within

My vision cleared as tiny particles of dust floated in the air around me, as the heartbeats of hundreds of people in the store flooded my ears, their thoughts, their souls in all their colors flashing for me to see.

I saw it all.

I saw the world through new eyes.

And I was greedy for more.

Serenity sucked through her lips and then fell back against the wall, mouth parted, blood dripping from her lower lip as her crazed green eyes met mine in confusion and wonder.

Chests heaving, we stared at one another.

I couldn't speak.

Slowly, I righted her clothes as she wiped her mouth and then in a stunned voice confessed, "You're half vampire."

I brought a shaking hand to my face and wiped my mouth. "How?"

"I don't have the power to change someone, to even awaken something that's been dormant. There's... there's no way. I'm not part of the council. I'm not old enough I'm—" She kept shaking her head.

"Cassius—" I grabbed her hand. "—Cassius will know. Let's grab the food and go."

"If the cart's still there." She shot me a small smile.

I returned it with a brilliant one of my own. "We were in a hurry."

"Next time…"

Did that mean there would be a next time? Could I even handle it without exploding on the spot?

"…we go slow."

"Slow," I agreed, not sure if I could do anything slow when it came to her. "We'll go slow."

I could have sworn I heard a dark chuckle from somewhere and a whisper that said, *"Lie."*

CHAPTER FIFTEEN

SERENITY

MY GUMS ACHED.

It started slowly like I'd bruised something in my mouth; the pain lessened then intensified so much that I was ready to press my hand against my teeth just to see if the agony would stop.

"What's wrong?" Mason's gravelly voice shook me out of my pain. "You're hurt." He said it like he knew it.

Like he knew me.

He reached over and grabbed my hand. The pain didn't stop, but it didn't increase again. I clenched his hand as tight as I could, my mind a whirlwind of impossibilities.

Impossible that he was half vampire.

Impossible that the blood I tasted on my tongue had my DNA.

Impossible that a half-wolf-half-vampire existed.

Impossible that he was my mate.

Impossible that we could mate.

He was a beast, a beast within a man, along with something other lurking beneath the surface — something he hadn't even faced in all of his centuries of living.

If he was afraid of what was inside...

Then I should be too.

And yet I held his hand. I squeezed it tight, and I felt the slow purr of breath escape between his lips, as if my touch made him happy.

Tears filled my eyes. So much uncertainty, so much we I didn't know, and so much I didn't want to know.

Because what if I'd just found someone to spend my eternity with — who would end up either rejecting me or hurting me in the process?

To my knowledge, immortals never mated in that way; they didn't cross breed. It was considered forbidden.

The only time I'd ever heard of anything remotely similar to it happening had been when angels bred with humans, creating Dark Ones, and look how wonderful that had turned out for everyone.

Mason snorted. "Tell me about it."

Crap.

He sighed as my tension increased in my shoulders. "I can only hear flickers of your thoughts, when you're really scared or upset. It's easy to pick out from a million other crowds, but I'm not good at it yet. Maybe—" He stopped himself.

"More blood," I answered for him. "Just imagine how powerful you'll be when you drink your fill."

The car chilled.

I shouldn't have said it.

His demeanor darkened right along with the sky.

And as torrential rain started slamming onto the windshield, I was left again with more questions than answers.

It was driving me insane.

I was about to ask him if he could pull over and give me a minute when something crashed into the car, sending us careening off the road and against a tree.

Mason turned his body my way, shielding me. It all happened in slow motion — the fear on his face, then determination as he wrapped his body around me before immediately morphing into a white wolf. His fur pressed against my skin as metal twisted around our bodies, and then an explosion of white enveloped us as our car disappeared, and a fallen walked right through, a look of curiosity on its angelic face.

"I was wondering…" Mason barked out. "…when you would sniff us all out. Curious?"

The fallen smiled; he was one of the Watchers, the ones who'd watched for a thousand years until the first angel fell, until Sarial created Cassius with his love for his human wife.

Until the twelve brothers who were set to watch over the human realm fell with them, allowing their eyes to shift from their purpose to the very ones they were supposed to be protecting.

The ones who watched had jet black hair with red shots throughout, as a mark to human or immortal that they were not fully angelic, not anymore.

The red was proof that they had to earn their spot back into heaven.

The black was proof they most likely never would.

A chained tattoo wrapped around his neck like a vice then rippled down his arm and coiled around each finger as if someone else was controlling him.

"Come, Gadreel." The fallen held out his hand. "Do you not recognize your brother?"

Mason shook his head and then gave out a sharp bark that sounded like a laugh, only with more teeth. "I'm clearly a wolf. You've been locked up too long. Making me regret even setting you free a few weeks ago. Aren't you supposed to be reporting to your archangel? The one who has you by the ass so you don't go to the bad place where they take your pretty feathers?"

The fallen closed his eyes. His lips began to move, and suddenly, Mason just collapsed right in front of me.

"What did you do to him!" I screamed, falling to my knees.

The fallen tilted his head at me. "I knew you would awaken him. Only one who can."

Fear trickled down my spine as he took a step closer, his eyes menacing. "We are stronger together. Cassius knows this. Better to ask forgiveness than permission."

"For what?" I knelt next to Mason, and he shuddered and gave a little howl before I pressed a hand to his fur. "What are you going to do?"

"Whatever it takes..." His teeth clenched. "...to go home."

He disappeared just like he'd come, leaving a chill so icy cold that I almost crawled into Mason's lap and shivered.

He moved to a sitting position, his eyes blazing blue

before he gave his head a shake and nuzzled my neck. "Are you okay?"

I nodded. "You?"

He didn't answer.

Maybe he didn't have to.

Nobody would be okay after that.

When I turned around to start walking, the Jeep was idling as if it hadn't just been rammed into a tree, as if we hadn't just had a visit from some creepy fallen angel with a revenge plan.

Mason eyed me then the car, and with a sigh said, "Get in."

We were five minutes away from the house when it set in. The burning, the need to bite him was so intense that my mouth started to water. The ache so great I was ready to lose my mind.

I focused on the trees we passed. Counted to a hundred.

And breathed a sigh of relief when we pulled up to the house.

"Don't tell them," Mason whispered.

I unbuckled my seatbelt. "Mason, you have to tell them. Something's going on, something big. You're — you're a hybrid. You have—" I left out the DNA part. "—you have vampire molecules in your bloodstream. That's not normal. What if it makes you more powerful?"

"What if..." He killed the ignition. "...it takes over completely?"

"It won't." I didn't know that for sure. I suddenly realized I didn't know anything. "Tell Cassius. He can help."

Mason shook his head and then pressed his lips together in a grimace. "Maybe. I don't..." He gave me a quick glance. "I felt him in me."

"Who?"

"The fallen, as if I knew him. He was probing me, speaking to me in a language I understood, and now I can't remember what he said."

"Maybe he was just trying to provoke you?"

"No." Mason's teeth clenched. "Trust me, that's not it."

He jerked the wheel to the side as we pulled up to the massive gate and into the driveway. A few vampires stood watch outside, looking more like bored GQ models than anything.

I got out of the car and flinched when one's gaze lingered on my face and then breasts too long for my liking. I was about to say something when Mason had him by the throat and pressed against the wall at least two feet off the ground.

"You as much as exhale six feet away from her, and I'll put your head on a spike and give you just enough blood to survive while I set wild dogs to your flesh!" Claws protruded out of Mason's hands, piercing the skin of the vampire's flesh, causing silver blood to drip down his skin. "Do we have an understanding?" Mason's voice deepened as huge fangs elongated from his mouth past his lower lip like he was getting ready for a midnight snack, and then his eyes glowed blue, only to go completely red as he leaned in.

"Mason!" Cassius barked. "That's enough."

Alex appeared in the doorway next, his smile smug. "Finally. Hungry, wolf?"

Hope peeked around Alex and moved toward Mason, but Alex put his arm out and gave his head a shake.

As if Mason was dangerous.

As if he'd hurt her.

Ethan and Genesis shared looks of concern.

And I was left wondering if I was even safe with Mason,

when neither of us knew what he was even capable of.

"Mason," Cassius said it again, "leave him."

Slowly, Mason shook his head as his eyes went back to a more piercing brown I was used to.

The vampire stumbled away while Mason pressed his hands to his head. "I'm sorry. I just—"

"Someone needs sex," Alex muttered.

Mason jerked his head toward Alex then gave him a shove, sending Alex careening back into the entryway and slamming against the wall with a crack. A few pictures fell, and a split grew in the wall.

Alex got up and dusted himself off. "That's gonna bruise in the morning."

"Mason. Alex." Cassius, the clear voice of reason shook his head and ushered everyone inside.

Timber was there. "I see it's progressing."

"Progressing?" Mason repeated. "What in the hell are you talking about?"

"He's bigger," Hope pointed out.

Alex scowled. "So he grew a few muscles."

Genesis whistled. "I'd say a few dozen at least."

Hope grinned. "Maybe more."

A sudden wave of heat blasted through the room, causing the freaking houseplant to shake and then combust.

"Was that necessary?" Cassius directed the question to Alex. "Take your jealousy elsewhere."

"I'm not jealous." Alex grunted.

Hope patted him on the shoulder and then leaned up on her tiptoes and kissed him. "You're cute when you lie."

"So…" Timber set down his coffee. "…are we going to talk about the elephant in the room first, or the immortal numbers and how the hell we're planning on wrangling up the ones who watch?"

"Elephant?" Mason looked genuinely confused. "Stop referring to me as an elephant. I'm a wolf. Calling me an elephant is an insult. It's like calling Alex ugly."

Alex rolled his eyes. "Thanks, man."

"I get you." Mason nodded and then flipped him off behind his back while Alex did the same back to Mason.

Cassius slammed his hands onto the kitchen table. "Children, all of you."

I could tell it was on the tip of Alex's tongue to say something like he started, but he held back. Instead, the room fell into a state of complete silence.

And then all eyes fell to me.

As if I was supposed to say something.

"What?" I whispered.

"Blood." Alex pointed at my t-shirt. "Curious." He searched the room. "Who exactly did you feed on at the grocery store? Some poor soccer mom trying to get last-minute dinner? A college student buying Top Ramen? A child?"

The more he spoke the worse I felt. The rage on his face wasn't for show.

"Me," Mason said, jerking everyone's attention to him. "She fed on me... but not before I fed on her."

CHAPTER SIXTEEN

MASON

I REGRETTED THE words as soon as they'd left my mouth. Hell, I'd even regretted them as I was saying them. Still didn't stop me from acting like an ass or stop everyone else from staring at me like I'd just grown an extra fang and tried to bite off Alex's head.

"What?" I shrugged, trying to appear calm when there was a tumultuous storm of emotion raging inside, fighting for dominance, pulsing with every pump of Serenity's blood. My mouth watered for her blood, for her taste. Could she tell? Could my family? Was it possible to see the need so etched within my soul that I was having a hard time concentrating?

I wanted to take her again and again.

My wolf wanted its mate.

Whatever vampire part of me just wanted blood.

And the other?

Well, that was the part I was afraid would awaken if I took more blood, if I actually had sex with Serenity — if the mating process was followed through to the end.

I'd already bitten her.

Twice.

If I was a vampire, we'd be well on our way to being mated; then again, she wasn't human — ergo, she wouldn't die without my blood.

And yet, I could see the thirst in her eyes when she'd suddenly glanced at my neck with such longing I wanted to fall to my knees and beg her to suck me dry.

"You—" Ethan jabbed a finger in my direction then frowned. "—not only let her feed off you, but… you fed…" He seemed to struggle with getting the word *fed* out. "…off her?"

"Monster. Monster. Monster." A voice inside me chanted.

It was wrong.

Something was wrong with me.

I gave a jerky nod.

"Was this before or after you guys did it in the produce aisle?" Alex asked in a bored tone.

I shot him a glare. "We didn't do it next to the produce."

"Oh, so the cereal then?" he asked.

"Alex!" Cassius' booming voice shook the house; his eyes darted to me. "The only way for you to have any breath of vampire DNA in your body would be if it was mixed with an angel's."

I gulped.

And then my mind raged as dark laughter filled my head.

An angel.

A fallen.

"Gadreel," a voice had whispered.

The room chilled as Stephanie entered. She looked between me and Cassius and then stopped. Her chest heaved with exertion as Cassius started speaking in an angelic tongue my wolf didn't — couldn't — understand.

And then...

My mouth tried to move.

I restrained myself. Barely.

"Allow it," Cassius said in a thick voice.

"No!" I roared.

Cassius gripped my throat. "You will never be free of this unless you face it."

"And if I never face it?"

"Then it will destroy you from the inside out." Cassius released me. "I never thought you were a coward."

Red filled my line of vision as I lunged for him.

He swatted me out of the way as if I was a fly buzzing around his head. I went sailing into the stainless-steel fridge and slumped against the ground.

"Mate," Cassius said in a voice that dared me to argue. "Am I your king, Mason?"

And there it was.

The room fell silent.

Shame washed over me.

Had it been so long ago? When I'd been revered as a king? As a leader over all the wolves? I'd led them through battles, through centuries of war, and there I was, on the kitchen floor, weak.

Defeated.

Starving.

Pathetic.

"Are you saying that someone mixed vampire blood with angel blood, and somehow got it into him?" Serenity asked in a small voice.

"It would appear so." Cassius shook his head. "I would have to go back in order to see..."

"Field trip." Alex rubbed his hands together.

Used to his antics, Cassius nodded and then held his hands out.

Serenity gaped at all of us.

I stood and pulled her to my side as Cassius pressed a hand to my head. The room stilled.

And we were falling.

My family.

Me.

Everyone in the room who had touched his wing.

When my eyes opened...

I wasn't in the kitchen anymore.

I was in my old home.

The one I'd been sent from.

I was in my castle in Scotland.

It was covered in blood.

CHAPTER SEVENTEEN

MASON

Shouting commenced as the doors to the stone castle shoved forward with great force. Standing there were two hooded figures, both of them imposing. Both of them... evil.

Everything about them felt wrong.

It felt... other.

My mom approached them, blood on her hands, her face pinched with worry and fear. My father stood behind her, his hand on her back.

"We can't..." My mom covered her face with her hands. "We fight amongst ourselves as much as we fight amongst the other immortals. They challenge us as king and queen. Every few years, we lose more and more of our armies. Our son has a sickness, one he was born with. It keeps him bound to his bed. My husband needs an Alpha to step in."

The hooded figure took a deep breath then rumbled in a low voice, "So, you've sought my help?"

My mom nodded. "I've heard what you can do."

The hood dropped from his face.

I swore as black hair fell around carved cheekbones, and one single strip of red placed in the front framed his angelic face. "Have you now?"

The person next to him laughed darkly.

Father held out his hand. "We have money, resources—"

"A favor." Bannick grinned menacingly. "All I ask is for a favor. I swear to you, you won't even be alive to follow it through."

Anxiety washed over me as my father held out his hand and shook Bannick's. "A favor. You have my word."

"I know." His grin was cruel, and then very slowly he tilted his head, closed his eyes, and breathed in before jerking his attention directly at me and whispering it again. "I know."

I backed away.

I could feel his stare through every inch of skin, bone, muscle.

"What you're doing..." Bannick slowly turned his attention back to my father. "...it is... not accepted." He pointed up to the ceiling. "It may get you killed, or your son, but if it works—war will stop. You'll have someone too strong, too powerful to challenge. An Alpha who is a hybrid like the world has never seen." He opened his mouth as if to say more then shut it. "Come, Gadreel. We'll need to hunt."

Father nodded. "I'll help."

Bannick outright laughed. "We can catch a silly vampire. It's getting them to agree that's the problem. But we have our ways… Everyone has a price, and I'm thinking I know just the vampire who's willing to do just about anything to have a child."

Time moved ahead of us in rapid succession as my body chilled. I reached for Serenity's hand only to discover she wasn't there.

I did a slow circle.

Completely alone, except for Cassius. He gave me a sad look. "It's not fair."

"What isn't?"

"To allow others in on our innermost fears, our thoughts." He put a hand on my shoulder. "I sent them back to the present. Let's see what they bargained for with the devil."

In the next scene I heard screaming first.

So much screaming.

It was my mother. She was hovering over me. "There's too much blood!"

"Not enough blood," Bannick said in a bored tone. "He needs to be bit a few more times."

The vampire glanced at my mother with green cool eyes and then continued attacking my small body.

I screamed at the top of my lungs as he took more blood.

"Stop." Bannick held out his hand. "Gadreel, come here, won't you?"

Gadreel stepped forward and then moved to his knees.

Bannick held a silver dagger in front of him. "If you ever fall, my brother, know that you will still exist in the next life stronger than before."

Gadreel peeled back his hood.

I wanted to turn away.

I wanted to run.

His eyes were ice blue.

His face matched mine exactly.

His hair was black with streaks of red, but other than that, he was an identical twin.

He smirked like he could see me.

I gripped the wall with my hands, clawed at it to keep from collapsing, and then Bannick shoved the blade into Gadreel's heart as silver blood spewed from the gaping hole onto the sharp weapon.

He held out the blade to my body and slowly dripped silver blood onto each bite wound, allowing the vampire to seal the blood in.

My small body convulsed as I moaned in despair.

It hurt.

Like being reborn.

Fire in my blood.

Ice in my brain.

A headache that refused to go away.

And a pulsing in my gums that begged me to ask for more.

Kill for more.

So confused.

My dark eyes darted toward my parents. The trust was broken. Gone. In its place only fear.

Fear that I'd somehow not been good enough. Strong enough.

And they'd do something so abysmal in order to make me...

Better.

Maither turned away and cried into my dad's chest as he

gave one final nod to Bannick.

His blade slid into my chest with precision.

Piercing my heart.

"Break the heart. Knit the blood. Feed the soul," Bannick whispered in an ancient tongue. "Your true identity will be forever hidden until *her.*"

The blade left my skin.

I didn't bleed.

Every single bite healed immediately.

I sat up straight. I looked murderous.

I went to grab the boy, the small boy who looked ready to kill the world, but Cassius held me back.

A crack of lightning lit up the room.

Followed by thunder.

Gadreel stood. "Looks like we pissed him off again."

"It's what we do best." Bannick shrugged. "At least then, we have his attention. We've been ignored too long. No more, brother. I've got plans for us. Big plans." Within seconds, they were gone.

The vampire finally turned toward us.

He looked familiar.

He gave his head a shake and then whispered in the air, "My want has blinded me."

Within minutes, another vampire walked in with a small child. "She's beautiful! The angels have stayed true to their promise!"

The girl immediately started to cry.

"What should we name her?" The male vampire held out his arms.

My mother chimed in. "Death. Name her death. For there is only death here." She collapsed against my father.

"She has only fainted," he explained, "and your daughter

is beautiful. Name her something that means peace."

The vampires nodded.

Seconds later, Sarial the archangel appeared.

And nothing was ever the same again.

Cassius gripped my shoulder. "There is nothing left to see that we don't know."

110

CHAPTER EIGHTEEN

SERENITY

ONE MINUTE I'D been in Scotland. The next I was back in the kitchen with Hope, Alex, Genesis, Stephanie, and Ethan. The twins were quietly sleeping upstairs, and the house creaked with awareness as if it knew magic had just occurred and wanted to tell the world its secrets.

Our secrets.

Another groan, and the house was silent again as wind whipped the trees in the yard, banging branches against the side of the house as a scratching noise kept my eyes locked on the sliding glass door leading to the expansive backyard.

"How safe are we here?" I wondered aloud.

Alex actually had the nerve to laugh and then immediately stopped when Hope smacked him on the chest. "Sweetheart, we're immortal. If any human—"

"Not from the humans." I felt the need to point out. "What about other immortals?"

Ethan frowned. "We have few enemies. We lead peaceful lives. The real enemy is the evil that was released a few months ago. Balance must always be restored, and the scale has been tipped in their favor."

"How so… exactly?" I asked.

"Bannick—" Ethan explained. "You saw him in the dream before Cassius kicked us out. He's thankfully chained in the abyss, but that doesn't mean his brothers aren't walking the earth, waiting for time to strike. They can't help it."

"What do you mean they can't help it?"

Ethan's eyes darted to Alex before answering. "Say you were born perfect, only exposed to one thing your entire life. You know of evil, but it never touches you. You know hunger, but have never felt it in your gut. You know pain, but have only ever been on the end that gives it. You've never truly suffered." He ran a hand through his long jet-black hair. "Then suddenly, you're thrown into a world that knows only pain, violence, war. The angelic heart is an interesting thing. It was only made for one purpose — to join with The Creator. When that joining was lost, when the twelve fell from the mountain, it severed that link. Tell me, if you were suddenly thrust into this world without half of your soul, would you not do anything to get it back?"

I suddenly had the need to sit. My legs hit the back of the chair as I plopped down. "So, they aren't evil? They're just willing to do anything to get back to their original state?"

"Pretty much," Alex chimed in. "And the last thing we

need is more fallen angels creating Dark Ones like Cassius — and Stephanie." He grinned at her, "No offense."

She rolled her eyes. "We can't have them exposing themselves to the humans, and they are desperate enough to do just that. Each of them have gifts, talents that if used for evil could bring along the apocalypse swiftly and violently." She looked away as the room dropped twenty degrees, ice particles suddenly appearing in front of my face. "They would kill every human on this planet, if it meant the link would be returned."

"Every human?" I repeated. "Even immortals?"

"Well, they could try." Alex winked, but his speech missed his normal sarcasm. Instead, fear appeared in his eyes as he very covertly pulled Hope into his arms and pressed his hands against her flat stomach.

My eyebrows shot up.

He gave me a single nod and then looked away like he too would kill every single human in the world — to protect his own.

A crack of thunder shook the house.

And suddenly, Mason was walking in like he'd just taken a stroll outside in nothing but low-slung jeans and enough muscle to enter a body-building competition.

Cassius followed, his purple wings tucked behind his back, his expression grim as he took in the scene around us.

"So good news then?" Alex joked.

Cassius reached for Stephanie's hand and kissed it before turning his attention to me. "Swear to me."

"What?"

His eyes blazed white. "Swear to me."

Mason moved toward us, but Cassius held his hand up as the room stilled, as if everyone was stuck in time except me and Cassius.

His wings spread out, making it impossible for me to escape. They rippled as a wind drifted through the house. Cassius reached for my face and cupped my chin with his right hand, the feathers on that wing shuddering like the touch was comforting. As if they were purring with each caress of his thumb. "Swear to me you won't look away."

"Look away from what?" I whispered.

"Him," he said quickly. "Where your eyes go, your feet will follow."

It sounded so familiar, that saying.

I frowned.

And then the room was back to normal. Mason charged toward me, shoving Cassius out of the way with such force the angel slammed into a wall.

"Oh, shit." Alex snorted out a laugh. "You been eating Wheaties or what?"

Mason's expression went from anger to horror. "Cassius, I'm sorry I don't—"

He cursed and ran up the stairs before Cassius could even say anything.

"I'll go." Hope kissed Alex on the cheek and ran after Mason.

Jealousy pierced my heart. It was wrong. I knew she was mated to Alex, but it didn't make it any easier to watch her go after Mason.

Alex sauntered over to me in that sexy way he had no control over and then sat down in the empty chair and stared me down. "So, you wanna bake cookies or something?"

"What?" I narrowed my eyes.

He jerked his head toward the stairway. "I bet he'd love warm cookies. He's more beast than man anyway — and if he doesn't like the snack, you can always offer your neck again. Seemed to work well the first time." His grin was dazzling. "I'll help, and you can tell me all about how hard it was growing up a sad, powerless vampire."

"How does she even live with you?" I wondered aloud, much to Genesis' and Ethan's amusement.

Alex grunted. "She wants me for my body, but can you really blame her?" His eyes changed color as his hair turned an orange blue.

"Cut it out, Alex." Ethan shoved him to the side. "You don't want to kill her. I'll grab the chocolate chips."

It wasn't the life I could have ever possibly imagined for myself. Making chocolate chip cookies with two of the most powerful immortals in existence while an archangel watched, his face a mask of worry. I almost missed the look he gave Genesis, the slow shake of his head, and the way her eyes filled with fear as if he'd just given her a warning only she would understand.

And when she went over to him and Stephanie, it wasn't to laugh and talk; it was to huddle in the corner and hold hands, as if it might be the last time any of them would see each other again.

CHAPTER NINETEEN

MASON

I sat in complete darkness on the windowsill. My gaze on the stars. Thousands of years ago, I'd asked to be the Great Wolf, without any regard to what that would mean.

And now?

Now it just felt like I was failing my parents all over again. All they'd ever wanted was for me to be powerful.

Instead, I was turning into a blood-obsessed freak, unable to control any of my emotions. The very fact I could shove Cassius, without putting effort into it, terrified me.

The fact that I could somehow sense the fear in that room — the anxiety — to the point where it wrapped itself around my neck and squeezed was wrong.

All of it was wrong.

Her heartbeat increased until I was afraid she was going to pass out, and then the sound returned to normal. I listened a bit longer, interested in the way my ears were able to pick hers out amongst all the different immortals'.

What was even more interesting — I heard Cassius' heart.

Felt it beat in my ears.

It was louder than the others. More powerful, but slower. Purposeful, like each beat was communicating something to the universe that none of us would ever get the privilege of seeing or understanding.

"Knock, knock." Hope shoved the door open and made her way toward me, her brown eyes sparkling.

"Why do humans say *"Knock knock"* instead of just knocking? And you didn't even wait for me to let you in." I crossed my arms.

Hope sat opposite me on the window and smiled brightly. She tugged at her plain black shirt and pressed a hand to her stomach briefly before answering. "First, it's more like *"Hey, I'm announcing that I'm coming in, and you can't stop me,"* and second, I didn't want to give you the opportunity to say no."

I growled.

"Oh stop." She scooted closer until I could feel the heat from her body. Her heart began to race.

I frowned down at her. "What?"

She licked her lips.

I pressed an ear to her chest and then jerked away, before slowly falling to my knees and pressing an ear to her stomach.

"How long?" I whispered, gripping her hips with my hands as I laid my head in her lap.

She ran her fingers through my hair.

I closed my eyes as warmth washed over me. I'd chosen well in a best friend.

She exhaled. "A few weeks. I told Alex yesterday. I had no choice. I puked all over him."

I chuckled. "I would have loved to have seen that. Filmed it. Looked at it every now and then when I'm tempted to rip his head from his body."

She gave me a light slap on the shoulder then kept playing with my hair. "I'm afraid."

I pulled back and gripped her hands. "Fear isn't weakness, Hope."

"It feels like weakness."

I stood and pulled her into my arms then led her to sit on the bed. It dipped under our weight. I brushed a kiss across her forehead. "Give me your fear then. I'll take it."

Tears filled her vision. "Elves used to die. That was their purpose, mate with an immortal then die after giving birth."

"You're not just an elf, Hope. You're the last. You're royalty. You can't die."

"How do we know that though?"

I hugged her tighter. "I know because Cassius says so, and I believe him. I trust him. He wouldn't ask you to mate only to have you lose one another. He isn't that cruel. Nobody is."

"But you lost your mate," Hope pointed out.

"Lost." I rolled the word around a bit. "*Lost* always seems like the wrong word. *Lost* means that she simply couldn't find her way back home and was taken. *Lost* seems like I did something wrong, that I couldn't keep her." I shook my head. "Maybe it is the right word. Maybe I never really had her. I was always too much for her, too strong, too big… too hairy."

Hope burst out laughing, "You aren't hairy."

"I'm a wolf. It's a compliment to be hairy. Could you imagine if I was bald?"

Hope made a face. "You'd be like one of those naked cats."

"Absolute demons, those cats. Hey, I've got a though. Let's get Alex one. I'll put a diamond leash on it, buy it a pillow—"

She slammed a hand over my mouth. "Don't you care!"

I licked her hand and winked. "Tell him to behave then."

"You guys are impossible." She crossed her arms. "Thanks for making me laugh. I know I'm being ridiculous. Here you are, trying to figure out why you keep wanting to bite people and being forced to mate again, and I'm complaining."

"We all have… things," I said simply. "Doesn't make any one of them less important. Don't compare problems because no matter what, to the person going through it, it will always seem impossible to solve."

She pressed a hand to my chest. "You said you trust Cassius, right?"

I nodded. "With my life."

Hope pulled away; the faint smell of vanilla filled the air as she locked eyes with me. "Then trust him in this. Don't lose Serenity as your mate. Keep her." Hope pressed a hand to my heart. "Trust that it's going to be okay."

I had been afraid to speak my fears aloud.

Afraid it would make them come true.

But it was Hope. My best friend since having run into her on the streets of London in the 1800s.

"What if it unleashes something I can't control?" I whispered. "What if I really am a monster? An other?"

"Look at me." Hope gripped my face with her hands. "It

won't happen. Your heart is good, Mason. You're good. This thing, you feel, this beast — maybe once you stop fighting it, you'll be able to control it by joining it."

I gasped.

"Stop fighting, Mason." She stood. "You've been fighting yourself so damn long, from joining your place with your pack to enjoying a freaking steak — stop punishing yourself for mistakes others made on your behalf."

"Mistakes?" I repeated, "What do you mean mistakes?"

"You're not too hairy. Or strong. Or any of those things. The biggest mistake your dead mate made was taking your love for granted. This is your second chance to be with someone who gets you."

I looked down at the ground. "I'll break her."

"She's a vampire. She can lift a car off a tree. I think she'll be okay." Hope winked then patted me on the back and walked off.

I lay back against the bed and sighed.

Little did Hope know I was way heavier than a car.

I smiled.

CHAPTER TWENTY

SERENITY

THERE WAS NO reason for my hands to be shaking, but they were. The warm cookies were barely staying stacked with on the plate. It was dark. And I'd just seen Genesis get in a car with the twins and Ethan and just leave; they had bags as if they were moving, but this was Ethan's house. My confusion only mounted when Cassius had whispered something to Alex that had him grabbing Hope by the arm the minute she'd reached the bottom of the stairs and pulling her toward the garage.

"Everything okay?" I'd asked Stephanie.

She'd only shrugged and had given me a funny look.

Cassius swept back into the room. "Remember what I said."

And that was it.

The house was dark.

And I was holding a stupid plate of cookies as if that was going to calm the beast in the upstairs bedroom — as if that was going to make him want me.

If your own parents don't love you enough to stay...

What makes you think that a plate of cookies is going to help an immortal king want to mate you?

That was the question I asked after every step.

After each breath.

What makes you so different?

Nothing.

Nothing at all.

Insecurity had a way of seeping into every crevice of my brain, making it impossible for me to come up with a scenario that had Mason choosing me, choosing us.

He barely knew me.

But his blood…

I briefly closed my eyes.

That wolf was made for me in ways I couldn't even begin to comprehend. Just thinking about him had my teeth aching, my body craving more.

I'd felt sick ever since the grocery store, and now I just wanted relief, relief only he could bring.

Mason.

The door was open.

I quietly walked in. Moonlight shone through the open window as cool night air filled the empty space between me and his massive body.

His breathing was slow.

His naked chest rose and fell with an easy cadence that immediately calmed me down.

I took a deep breath and then approached.

I didn't even have time to speak before his hand snaked out and gripped my free hand.

"What…" He leaned up on his elbow. "…is that smell?"

I cleared my throat. "Cookies."

"Cookies." His icy gaze locked on me.

"Chocolate chip cookies." I couldn't tear my eyes away from his, from the way they penetrated every defense without asking permission to do so. His eyes stripped me bare without a thought.

I let them.

My body heated.

He dropped my hand and reached for a cookie. "I haven't had a cookie in…"

"Years?" I offered.

His mouth curved into a sultry smile. "Hundreds."

"That's some hardcore self-control," I joked.

His smile was tense. The room swirled. It pulsed with electricity, with blood that pounded my body, begging for release, begging to be joined with his.

White teeth bit into the cookie slowly. My eyes followed as his tongue snaked out and licked a bit of chocolate that had the honor of grazing his perfect, plump lower lip. My mouth buzzed with jealousy. I would probably slit someone's throat to be that piece of chocolate.

Mason closed his eyes and let out a guttural groan before reaching for another cookie.

Repeating the process.

While I died a thousand deaths imaging those teeth biting into my soft flesh, licking me dry.

He reached for another.

And another.

The plate was empty.

Mason popped one final piece in his mouth then slowly sucked each finger dry. A piece of chocolate was on the corner of his mouth. The temptation was too much. Without asking permission, I leaned forward and swiped my tongue across the spot, tasting him, tasting the chocolate.

He stilled.

I whispered against his mouth. "Did you want milk?"

His hands gripped my waist.

It was a heartbeat, the second of indecision on his face warring with his duty, with his self-control, and just like that, I saw him finally give in, finally just...

Combust.

"I have a better idea," he growled.

Thank God.

My jeans scratched my skin as he roughly shoved them down to my ankles like going slow was never a first option.

Only one speed.

One way to claim.

My heart raced as his rough hands ran down my bare legs. I stepped out of the jeans and kicked them to the side.

His mouth pressed a kiss to my thigh. His hands dug into my skin as if he was afraid I was going to run away.

"I won't know how to stop," he said in a gruff, animalistic voice I recognized as his wolf — the animal inside him. It didn't terrify me.

It made me crave.

"Then don't," I encouraged as he picked me up and threw me against the bed as if I weighed a pound, when I knew vampires weren't known for being light or easy to throw.

I was a feather.

Putty in his hands.

He grinned down at me. And then started a full-on assault with his mouth as he licked and sucked my tongue until my only choice was to use his air for survival and cling to him with my hands.

His heart skipped a beat when I kissed him back, and when my tongue touched his, I could have sworn I heard his heart stop all together as blood rushed through his body hardening against me, making me squirm beneath him with primal need.

"Mine." I gripped his ass through his jeans then tried to shove them down.

He growled against my neck, his muscles strained as he held himself above me. His eyes went so light blue I could almost see my reflection in them. I squeezed him with my hands, pressing another kiss to his open mouth, cutting his lip on my fang.

He jerked back and then shuddered as what looked like an orgasm ran through his body, and then I felt it, what he was feeling, this insane need...

To feed.

Slowly, I turned my head to the side and moved my hair.

"Damn it, Serenity—"

"Take it," I begged. "Take me."

His breathing slowed, and then his hand was on my neck, more claw than fingers.

I wasn't afraid.

His eyes flickered from black to blue, over and over again as he watched me move beneath him. A war raged inside my mate's body.

"Let me set you free," I pleaded.

He let out a roar so ear-piercing that the house shook with it.

I almost looked away but then remembered Cassius' words as Mason's fangs descended like sharp swords coming from his mouth.

They were longer than mine, menacing.

I waited for him to strike — to take.

He didn't.

He watched me watch him.

I tried my best not to blink to show him I wasn't afraid, to be worthy of both man and beast.

His length strained against my thigh, and I moved beneath him. His eyes were crazed as he lowered his head between my legs and nuzzled, as if he was going to take a really arousing nap.

My thighs clenched while he ran his nose along every bare inch of me, his tongue outlining and pulsing with increased movements. He kept his claw on my neck, making it impossible to move.

He trailed slow dangerous circles with his tongue, only to stop as my body pleaded for release. I tried to move with him, but every time I did, he would stop what he was doing. Since I needed him to keep going, since it felt like my life depended on his touch, his every lick, I closed my eyes and let the rapture of his mouth fill my body.

His appetite seemed to only increase the more my body gave way as hot waves of pleasure shot through my core.

The process would repeat as he licked me up again and again. With a hungry growl, he feasted and then stopped as a pinch of pain hit my inner thigh.

The world stilled.

Silence.

His heavy breathing…

My stuttered heart…

The claw holding me still dug into my flesh.

I whimpered at the contact and felt his tongue lick the wound dry before he returned his attention to me.

My mouth…

My neck…

His eyes darted from my skin to my lips as if he wasn't sure which he should taste first, as if it was the hardest choice he'd ever made in his entire life.

The struggle was still there, but I could see logic return to his expression as he tried to calm himself down.

But I didn't want him calm.

That wasn't Mason.

Mason was all beast.

And I wanted him to know that I wanted both beast and man.

How could I not?

I met his gaze and then pushed his claw into my neck, piercing my own flesh enough for blood to trail down my white skin.

And realized too late…

That I'd just unleashed the beast.

And thrown away the key.

CHAPTER TWENTY-ONE

MASON

I'D STRIPPED HER millions of times in my mind.

Nothing was as good as this feeling.

This taste.

Like spending an eternity eating pinecones and suddenly having a dozen chocolate cookies spread out for me to feast on.

I feasted her.

I let my tongue eat her as if she was my meal.

And when I felt her blood soar, muscles clench, body react, my beast was satiated — for seconds — before it needed to feed again.

Each wave came harder and faster, my own body aching with the need to join her, but I'd been starving.

Living a life in the desert.

I'd been brought to a palace.

I wanted to feel everything.

My fangs pricked her inner thigh, and as blood coated my fang, I swallowed on instinct and felt a roaring in my chest that sounded like thousands of years of oppression.

Millennia of being shut out.

Lost to the world.

Sleeping.

I opened my eyes.

And saw it all, the way her heart sang to me.

Turning back now would have been impossible.

I would rather have died.

Her half-lidded gaze locked on mine before she clung to my feral hand and slit part of her throat open.

Opened her vein...

To the beast.

Without thinking of the consequences.

I threw my head back and roared as her blood ran down her neck and across her collarbone. With a growl, I struck at the vein and sucked.

It wasn't enough.

Warm blood coated my dry mouth as my body lit up from the inside out as if I'd never truly been alive until this point.

She bucked against my body, rubbing her sex against me like she needed it just as much as I did.

I pulled back long enough to flip her onto her stomach, and then my teeth were at her neck again, sucking, licking, devouring every inch of blood she offered, knowing I would never be the same.

I would never come back from this craving.

This lust.

She thrust her ass against me as I drank deeper; her arm came up behind her to cradle my head tenderly, her body moving back against mine.

Claim.

Claim.

Claim.

Her blood chanted.

Thunder boomed in the distance.

With shaking hands, I gripped her hips and pulled her back onto me, sliding all the way in, staying there, never leaving again.

Home.

Her scream was one of ecstasy.

My grip was one of power as I claimed my mate, as I made her mine while she moved with me.

"Enough," a voice whispered.

I pulled my mouth away from her only to have her latch onto my wrist as I continued my steady thrusts.

The feel of her teeth against my flesh was too much at once, to know she was mine, to know she wanted me; she wanted my taste, my blood to soar in her veins.

I found my release quickly, and her head fell back against my chest as blood dripped from her mouth.

And slowly, her heartbeat stilled.

And matched mine.

An invisible thread appeared in my mind, between us, never to be severed. And I could have sworn I heard angels singing.

I heard creation in her heartbeat.

I tasted it on my tongue.

And when I licked her wound closed on her neck, I cradled her face and gasped as her eyes lit up with blue. Just like mine.

They were wide, her eyes.

They were also... afraid.

CHAPTER TWENTY-TWO

SERENITY

"Don't look away."

"Don't look away."

My body was still buzzing with his presence. I felt him everywhere, tasted even more.

But the man I was looking at...

I wanted to look away from.

Because I saw death in his eyes.

I also saw life.

I saw things he shouldn't have been.

I saw things that were impossible to see.

I saw my own shame. I saw my faults. I saw everything

that made me a bad vampire, a bad person. I saw histories and deaths. I saw diseases, destruction. I saw war.

Trust. I needed to trust Cassius.

But I had a bad feeling that I hadn't just mated with Mason.

But a fallen.

CHAPTER
TWENTY-THREE

MASON

T HE AFTERMATH.

The awareness of her body was like a balm to my heart.

It was also the only reason I wasn't yelling at the top of my lungs, the only reason I wasn't cursing Cassius into the abyss.

Other. My. Ass.

I was no more *other* than Cassius was honest.

I gave my head a shake.

I wanted to be wrong.

But I saw her face.

It was not the face of trust. It was the face of fear.

"Serenity." Even my voice sounded different to my own ears; everything had heightened from the way the air shifted and shaped words into existence to the power I felt at even uttering them.

Ultimate power.

I craved it like I craved her.

"Mason?" She said my name like a question.

"Yes?" I answered the only way I knew how as confusion filled my head, my heart.

"Do you... do you know what's going on?"

I shook my head. "I know you're mine. That is what I know."

The house shook with my statement, and I could hear the very earth roar to life, as if it was waiting for me to create, to call something into existence.

I didn't feel evil.

But I felt evil all around me, tempting me, telling me to give in, so that I could be free.

Serenity took a deep breath and pressed her hands onto my shoulders. "We need Cassius."

"Why?" I tilted my head; the motion felt funny, but I'd just drunk my body weight in blood. Wolves didn't do that.

Very slowly, Serenity dipped her hands into my hair and tugged it forward. I almost vomited all over the bed when I saw the locks in her shaking hands.

Black.

And.

Red.

CHAPTER
TWENTY-FOUR

SERENITY

He sounded like Mason.

My heart recognized his heartbeat.

What I was seeing was impossible.

And yet, I'd just mated with a werewolf. As a vampire, I could suspend disbelief to an extent.

Mason kept looking at his hair, then he jumped from the bed to look in the mirror in all his naked glory.

I tried not to stare.

It was next to impossible.

He was perfectly formed, like a sculpture you see in a museum; every ounce of tissue on his body was sinewy muscle, rock-hard, from his tree-trunk legs to his flat abs. Scars marred his back, scars that I'd never seen before. Black hair ran down to the middle of his spine.

Red sliced through the black on either side, creating highlights brought on by blood.

Slowly, I stood and wrapped a sheet around my body.

The minute I approached, he tugged the sheet down and looked his fill, his eyes achingly slow as they drank my body in.

"I want you again," he whispered. "But—"

"Take me." I was his, and he was mine — no matter what color his hair, his skin.

He grinned. "I like your thoughts. They make me think this is just… an odd coincidence of a werewolf and vampire mating."

I gulped. "I wish that were the case, but—"

"But then I wouldn't know how to make that tree die out there." He nodded toward the window. "I wouldn't know the exact phrase to use to speak to the grass so it grows. I wouldn't know those things, no."

He was easily over a foot taller than I, and I reached up and touched the scars on his back only to stutter back when a black feather suddenly appeared and fell to the ground at my feet.

The minute I touched it, it disintegrated into ash.

Mason swore and then shoved me behind him so hard I almost collided with the mirror.

"What is it?" I whispered.

He shook his head in disbelief. "Well, it looks like I won't need to go hunting for them."

"Them?"

"Watchers," he whispered and then uttered deep in his

throat a scratchy, "My brothers."

CHAPTER TWENTY-FIVE

MASON

My jeans barely fit over my massive body. The minute I put on my old shirt, it ripped across my chest like a bad super-hero movie.

I was used to being shirtless but this felt... different. As if I was standing on holy ground and would get struck down for not having enough clothing on.

Serenity gave me a terrified look before quickly redressing. I wanted to take her fear, all of it, and make it go away.

But when I was the very thing she had been taught to fear?

Like every immortal out there?

What then?

It was a mistake; it had to be.

I felt my wolf growl within.

I was still a wolf.

I was still me.

And yet, I *wasn't.*

I didn't know how to process what was happening to my body as my thoughts went a million miles a minute only to focus once more on Serenity. "I protect what's mine."

A knock sounded at the door.

I was more worried that they were knocking than if they'd just appeared out of nowhere.

I gripped Serenity's hand and walked down the stairs to the front door, then jerked it open too hard, causing it to come off the hinges.

Hell.

Ethan was gonna be pissed.

"Gadreel," the man said. The name that fell from his lips was the same one that one of the Watchers had said to me during the car accident, as if I had someone or something trapped inside of me, and he'd been waiting for me to set it free.

I shivered and kept Serenity behind me as I stared him down, waiting for something, anything. My hesitation was short-lived when his name was pushed into my brain like someone had shoved a giant object past my eyes that read *Armaros.*

I gulped and then whispered, "Armaros," testing the way it sounded in the air.

His lips parted, and then he hung his head as if he'd been waiting a million years to hear his name released into the universe.

He raised his eyes and tilted his head in a predatory way as the men behind him watched, waiting, it seemed, for him to move, to do something. "Do you... remember?"

I didn't want to remember.

I didn't want to know.

My wolf cried out.

No. It would hurt too much.

My body had already suffered greatly; my mind was just barely hanging on by a thread. I'd lived thousands of years alone. I'd lost. I wasn't sure I could handle someone else's memories, the memories of what it would feel like to be one with creation — then the feel of it being ripped from my very hands.

"I don't want to," I said honestly.

"You..." He lifted his hand as his eyes flashed silver. "... have no choice."

The minute his palm pressed against my forehead, a chill washed over my body, and then I was on a mountain in the bitter cold, frost coating my lips as my heart slowed to a normal rhythm.

I watched.

I was one who watched.

I watched the humans.

I protected the mountain.

My job was to watch.

A war broke out.

"NO!" a woman screamed. "Help us!" She looked to the mountain, to us, her protectors, but it was not our job to intervene.

And then, a flinch.

The howling of a wolf was our only warning, and then a second, followed by several more.

Do. Not. Do. This.

The creator will never forgive you.

A decision.

My body shook as one of us, Sarial, took a step forward. Setting his eyes upon the children being thrown into the fire by the enemy. "We must stop this."

"Our job is to watch," another brother said. "And watch we will."

I found myself taking a step forward.

Armaros put his hand on my shoulder.

The howling intensified.

And slowly, one by one, my brothers and I began charging down the mountain. We slaughtered them all; the enemies blood coated my sword and gold breastplate. I felt nothing but anger.

Resentment.

I felt.

And I had never felt before.

I did not know how to deal with this emotion filling my lungs, making it hard to breathe.

And as I walked back to my spot on the mountain, I knew our lives were never going to be the same, for we'd taken our eyes off our purpose. And there would be hell to pay for it.

Sarial was the last.

I watched him talk to a woman. I watched him touch her.

I shuddered, wondering what that touch would feel like. Would it be warm? Cold? I looked away.

We all turned a blind eye.

I could feel Bannick's rage on the other side of me, but it wasn't one of war. It was jealousy.

He had his eye on the woman like she held the world's secrets.

No, things would never be the same again.

And days later, when Sarial slept with the woman, when they produced the world's first Dark One — we were punished.

I cried out as lightning split the sky in two, as black snow began to fall across my face, as The Creator once and for all looked upon us, and then turned away.

And his turn caused darkness to descend like a choking blanket around each and every one of us.

I ripped at my armor.

Pried it from my body so I could breathe.

"He's gone." Armaros fell to his knees. "The Creator has left us."

"Our punishment was not as severe as it should have been," I whispered.

I watched as Bannick took to the skies, his white wings carrying him higher and higher to the heavens until he started to fall.

I gasped in horror as his body increased speed then hit the ground with earthquake-like severity, and when I ran over to him to help, all I saw was black broken wings.

And redder in his hair, as if his defiance had caused The Creator to mark him for death.

"There is only one thing we can do," Armaros said, turning away. "We earn our way back, whatever it takes, guard the human plane as The Creator has asked. We must be vigilant in watching. We must not look away."

Bannick stood and shouted at the heavens, then he fell to his knees again and cursed The Creator to the abyss.

"It may be too late for some of us," I whispered.

The vision shifted, and suddenly I was in a small hut with Armaros staring me down like I'd done something unforgivable. Maybe I had. A thousand years had passed, and still no word from The Creator.

Not even when I'd built altars for him.

When I'd praised his land.

When I'd built up forests with my bare hands, made trees sing his name.

I'd hunted with the wolves, helped them feed their young, interacted with the Alpha as if he was my own kind.

They were favored among The Creator, built from his very hands, their flesh kneaded by the very trees and dirt they protected. The protectors of earth, I honored them, and he still refused to honor me back.

I may as well be dead.

I took a seat opposite Armaros.

His eyes narrowed, and then he flinched. "What have you done, brother?"

"Nothing that can be undone." I shrugged and took a seat as Bannick waltzed in with a victorious smirk like I'd actually given in to his evil ways.

Armaros shifted his attention back to me. "Do not listen to him."

"So, I should listen to you?" I yelled. It was all for show; it always was when it came to Bannick, but he didn't need to know that. Only Armaros truly knew me, knew my soul desire to create not destroy. "I have everything I need here."

"Yes." Armaros sighed. "We rule dust and destruction. How lovely for us, and how benevolent of him, right, Bannick?"

Bannick slammed his hand onto the table between us. "Don't you see? We will be here suffering for millennia."

"Our job is to guard the human planes," Armaros said carefully. "If we do our job, The Creator will honor us."

He'd been saying the same damn thing since the dawn of time. And still.

Silence.

Heavens above, I was disgusted with silence.

"The Creator doesn't even answer your song anymore, Armaros, most favored! Do you think for one second he would return the rest of us?" Bannick snapped.

Armaros looked away.

I felt shame over me. What I'd done was wrong.

I'd prayed in that moment, as the blade had pierced my heart — for The Creator to take me home.

I'd wanted to die.

I'd tried everything but the forbidden way to help take my own life — to give life — as was The Creator's only job. I'd taken his job in hopes he would look my way; he would see that I was committing the ultimate sin.

But it had actually worked. I had not died, and the boy would grow strong. And for that, I would have some peace at least during of my miserable existence.

"One day…" Bannick charged off. "…one day, you'll see."

Armaros shared a look with me and then whispered. "Let me see your chest."

I flinched with pain.

Why was I in pain?

I'd never felt pain before, but I knew that was what this was, this feeling.

I dropped to my knees as silver blood began spewing from the wound on my chest.

Armaros caught me before I hit the ground. Light filled

the room, and my shame grew with every passing second. "I know what you've done."

The voice was gentle.

It wasn't booming.

It held no judgement.

Just truth.

I closed my eyes.

"Open," the voice commanded.

A small boy stood before me, his face glowing with light.

I reached for his hand.

He took a step and then allowed me to feel him, to feel his warmth.

"Bannick means this for evil, what you have done." He grinned. "But I am The Creator, am I not? I see all? Know all? I let my children choose."

"Yes," I croaked. "You are. You do."

Armaros shook beside me. It was the only logical reaction to something so good, so fiercely terrifying even angels shuddered in his presence. Had I still had my wings, they would be dripping with blood, in pain at his beauty.

"So, you may choose now." He put a hand on my shoulder. "You can stay with your brothers here, guarding the planes, or you can die, your soul will be united with mine, but your body will be forfeited to another. Never again will you walk with your brothers on this plane, never again will you watch. But you will be whole."

It was the final thread. He would severe the final link between me and my brothers. The only thing that kept us sane was each other and our creator. And now he was offering me him, but without them.

How could I choose?

"Why?" I shook my head. "Why would you gift me with

this after what I've done?"

HIs smile was blinding. "Because my plan is much bigger... than you."

Tears filled Armaros' eyes. "Go, brother. Go."

"But—" I shook my head. "—those who watch... We all have a human plane to watch. It's... it is our duty, our punishment. I cannot part from you!"

Armaros stood tall. "I will watch for you."

Tears filled my eyes. I knew the toll I was asking him to endure just so my soul could return, the pain my brothers would suffer when my consciousness was taken from the fold. It would be an empty hole in their hearts for the rest of their lives.

"Go," He said it again, urged me.

I looked to the creator and gave him a single nod.

And felt nothing but peace.

"You will see him again," The Creator whispered in the air, "but he will not be the same. He will need to make a choice just like the rest of you. But the immortal is powerful. He is... a Great Wolf. A warrior. He will do Gadreel proud."

Armaros nodded.

And the vision faded.

I stumbled backward as Armaros' eyes returned to a pale blue, and then he held out his hand and pressed it against my shoulder. "Welcome home, brother."

I collapsed at his feet.

And howled.

CHAPTER TWENTY-SIX

SERENITY

I REACHED FOR Mason, but Armaros stopped me and gave his head a slight shake. "He may hurt you."

"He—" I pointed down at a shaking Mason. "—is my mate!"

Armaros stumbled back and shook his dark hair; pieces of red lit up the tips. "That is impossible, you're a..." He made a disgusted face like I was beneath him. "...a vampire."

"Thank you, I wasn't aware," I said sarcastically.

"No," Armaros whispered, "you don't understand. What you are saying is... it is impossible!" He knelt by Mason and then offered him a hand. Each of the men were huge, from their black and red hair, to the worn jeans and shirts that looked way too small on them. Jackets covered their muscles, and tattoos lined their arms.

The tattoos that peeked out from Armaros arms were angelic markings in an ancient tongue few understood or dared speak aloud for fear they would be struck dead.

"I love her," Mason's gruff voice sounded. "She is my mate. She is the reason this happened to me!" He gripped his hair and looked down at his massive body as if it wasn't incredible. A gift from The Creator for sure.

He had been beautiful before; his eyes had always held a certain fierceness, a deep-rooted sadness.

But now? Now he looked glorious.

"Angels do not mate with humans or immortals," Armaros said in a deadpan voice. "What you have done will get you killed."

A sudden chill filled the air as Stephanie stepped through the giant men and winked. "Maybe tell that to Cassius then."

And like a bomb hitting the ground, Cassius landed between them in perfect movie-star fashion, his purple wings spread wide, nearly taking out a few of the men before he tucked them back and stood.

"Cassius," Armaros spat.

"Saved your ass." Stephanie said through clenched teeth. "Or is your memory that crappy? If it hadn't been for us, all of you would still be chained to a damn wall getting bled to death by your brother!"

"Do you think this is any better!" Armaros shouted. "We have no purpose! We wander the earth as prisoners still! There may not be a wall, but, my friend, I am still very much chained!"

Cassius sighed and shared a look with Mason before

addressing Armaros. "The balance between creation and the humans must be restored. Every second of the day you choose to wander instead of returning to the planes you guarded is another day of chaos! Earthquakes, hurricanes, death, destruction. The universe is not balanced!" Cassius' voice shook the house. "And that is on you!"

"We," Armaros sneered, "do not report to The Creator anymore, or have you forgotten? The way that he has?"

"He never forgets," Cassius whispers. "It's how he forces us to learn."

"For thousands of years?"

"Not my fault you're stubborn." Cassius grinned.

Armaros looked ready to kill him.

"You could try," Cassius said through clenched teeth.

"What promise can you give us that The Creator will return us to our rightful place?" he asked calmly.

"I can't." Cassius shrugged. "It's called faith."

Armaros moved like he'd been struck while the rest of the brothers began whispering amongst themselves.

"By all means, take your time," Cassius said under his breath.

Armaros shared a look with Mason that looked skeptical. It held... a challenge.

"The wolf has Gadreel's body. He has his memories. He does not have his personality."

"Thank you," Mason grumbled.

"I wasn't complimenting you." Armaros lifted a shoulder while Mason looked ready to rip his head off. "It has been since the beginning of time that the angels have united with immortals without war, without evil."

"Yes," Cassius agreed, his eyes searching Armaros, "you're correct."

"A truce… between all of us." He looked to Mason. "But I want a link to the wolves."

Mason's eyes widened as if he'd just asked for his head. "But that's—"

Cassius held up his hand. "You want the connection to the heavens they provide?"

A single nod. "I want the music. I want the taste of the words on my tongue. Link us to the wolves, and we'll return to our planes."

Cassius sighed and looked straight at Mason. "You'll have to ask their rightful king."

And then Cassius did the strangest thing I'd ever see an angel do. He took a knee right in front of Mason and held his hands high.

Mason jerked back against me, as if he wasn't ready.

Words like *undeserving*.

The Creator will not communicate with me.

I can't do this.

Lost my mate.

Lost everything.

Lost everything. Can't lose her too.

I gripped his hand and squeezed.

And slowly, one by one, the Watchers bent a knee in the same way.

"Why are they bowing?" I whispered.

Mason sighed. "Because the only way for them to honor The Creator without the link to the heavens is to do it through the one who was created by the palm of his hands."

CHAPTER TWENTY-SEVEN

MASON

THE WATCHERS.

My brothers.

Gadreel's brothers — they all left.

I watched the fire crackle and spit while Serenity made me another batch of cookies. I could feel her anxiety through that invisible thread that mating created. She needed to do something.

And she understood nothing.

Vampires weren't often told about the werewolves' origin. It wasn't their typical bedtime story. If it had been they'd feel inferior, and wolves always kept to themselves.

Every immortal had a purpose.

We were capable of supernatural healing as a gift from The Creator; it came directly from him, the power.

The smell of cookies filled the living room until my mouth watered, and when she brought me a plate, I couldn't take it fast enough.

I was mid-bite, when Serenity spoke. "What did they mean when they said it was impossible for us to mate?"

I finished the cookie and swallowed the last of it then turned to her. "Mortal enemies?"

"That's not even true, and you know it." At least she smiled.

I pulled her into my lap just as Cassius swept into the room and sat.

I gave him a glare that would have sent anyone packing.

It only seemed to amuse him more as he stole one of my cookies, popped it in his mouth, and reached for another. I growled. He still took it.

He was lucky I liked him and didn't bite his head off.

"So…" Cassius leaned forward. "…I assume all the puzzle pieces fit now?"

Serenity blushed bright.

I clenched my teeth.

"Oh, not those. I knew those would, er… fit." He moved in his seat as if he were uncomfortable then smiled. "I meant your need for blood, your need to feed, to taste, to fill."

"Vampires…" I said the word softly. "gave me blood, and because it would never stay within my body and keep me healthy, they used angelic blood to bond it into my body, enough blood to kill Gadreel, to give me his essence."

"More or less." Cassius shrugged. "Which is why we were so concerned when Bannick was trying to do this again with his brothers, and yet every host kept dying... every human, every immortal. Alex would have been strong enough, but he was nothing compared to you." Cassius face turned grave. "You were but a child, a bairn in your mother's arms."

I smiled at his use of bairn.

"He should have died?" Serenity asked.

"Adult immortals would have suffered greatly, but the vampire blood mixed with werewolf blood..." He shrugged. "Why do you think it is frowned upon for immortals to mate?"

Serenity rolled her eyes. "Immortals would die off if they tried mating with one another. There are never children."

Cassius stood and gave us a funny look. "Oh, but there was one."

"What?" Mason slid the plate away from Cassius. "Who?"

Cassius looked between myself and Serenity and whispered. "Guess."

CHAPTER
TWENTY-EIGHT

SERENITY

I JUMPED TO my feet. "No. That's impossible! I'm young! I've only been alive three hundred years or so!"

Cassius stared.

Mason gripped my hand.

"No." I shook my head. "My father was an immortal. He found my human mother…" Her voice trailed as Cassius' eyes grew sad.

He approached, his wings spread. They quivered and then started to drip with tears. "Are you ready for your truth?"

Fear slammed into my chest. I rubbed it away with my hand. "No."

Cassius grabbed my hand. "You were created for evil."

Mason growled low in his throat.

"But what was meant for evil... turned out for good." He released her hand and walked toward the fire. "You'll see your truth in the flames, Serenity. When you're ready."

He disappeared.

I squeezed my eyes shut.

Mason wrapped a blanket around me then pulled me up onto the couch. "Movie or flames?"

"Movie," I said immediately.

He turned on *The Lion King,* not my first choice.

And I could have sworn he thought he was an actual lion. When he saw antelope, he'd move his head like he was getting ready to strike. I didn't miss he few times his claws came out, and he pawed the air like he was ready for attack.

I pressed my lips together to keep from laughing and lost it when he started to purr; the gravely sound felt like home. I pressed my head to his chest and giggled more when the vibrations tickled my ear. "Still wolf."

"Still wolf," he said softly. "I'll always be a wolf even if I do have Gadreel's memories and apparently, his knowledge of creation."

"Do you think you have his power?"

"I'm afraid to see," he said simply. "But I feel something buzzing beneath my skin, though it could be because my arm fell asleep around a half hour ago from you lying on it."

I jerked away.

He smiled and then tugged me closer.

I gripped his dark hair with my hands and pulled his mouth down to mine. I kissed his lips, tasting the chocolate still there from all two dozen cookies he'd devoured in one sitting. With a moan, he flipped me onto my back and spread his hand wide across my chest, nuzzling my neck with his nose before sucking my bottom lip, his fangs grazing my skin with such tenderness I wanted to cry.

He'd driven me crazy with his aggression, and now he was driving me wild with his slow burning passion. The way he tilted my head at the perfect angle so he could suck my lips and press kisses to my eyelids like they needed attention just as much as my mouth.

There wasn't one inch of space that he didn't claim. Every kiss was given with tenderness, with care, with this deep-rooted love that I'd never felt before. I thought I'd known love with my parents.

Then why did I finally feel whole with him?

With this man who'd taken a stranger into his arms and healed her without question?

I choked back tears as he nipped at my neck, a slight sting, and then I felt him suck. I groaned as he moaned against my vein, as if it was his favorite place to be. As if I was the home he'd never had until now.

His hands gripped my jeans once more, tugging them away until they fell to the floor, and as more clothes joined them in a pile, my body burned for his, so hot for his touch that I couldn't catch my breath.

"You're so beautiful." He cupped my face. "It was my very first thought when I saw you."

"You mean underneath all the scratches and dirt?" I joked.

He didn't smile. "Scratches and dirt can't hide true beauty, Serenity."

My heart squeezed as he dragged his mouth down my collarbone and pressed a kiss to my chest as he cupped my breasts and bit again.

I'd never felt such an erotic bite in my entire life. The soft flesh pierced with his fangs. His head moved across my breast. The vision was perfect. He was perfect.

He looked up. "I want to watch you this time."

"Watch me?" I frowned.

"I want to take you." His shirt ripped as he tried to pull it over his head.

I laughed at his irritated expression then stopped laughing altogether when his hips rocked against me, his length pressing close enough that I could feel its heat pulsing, waiting for me. "This way, where I can see your eyes."

"Is that not normal?"

"Not for wolves."

"Well, good thing it is for vampires." I laughed as I tugged his mouth down and kissed him with all the desperation I felt in my soul whenever he looked at me like I was the only one who existed in the universe.

He pulled back and pierced my lip with a fang. "Good thing I'm both."

"Yeah, good thing." I winked as he descended again, this time pressing into my core so deliberately slow that my body shook with the feel of it.

Long, even movements he watched, his gaze intense on my response, on my form, as he moved this hand between our bodies. I let out a gasp as he pushed me farther toward the edge, using my expressions to change his speed, his angle, driving me crazy with the way he was able to read my eyes and my body's response to his.

I ran a hand down his chest. My gums ached to taste him.

He moved his hand across my lips, knocking my fangs on his skin. I sucked in his sweet and smoky blood, my eyes locking on him while he moved inside me, while he claimed me as his again and again.

His teeth clenched. And then he was glowing again, his eyes so light blue, and then an icy white like the rest of the Watchers I'd seen that day.

For one brief second, I saw heaven in his arms.

I felt the way his soul longed for it.

And then the strangest thing happened. When he looked down at me, his feelings intensified as if his soul recognized that maybe heaven wasn't in the sky.

But in his arms.

"You..." He held my shaking body. "...you're my heaven. A gift from The Creator."

I nodded through my tears. "Yours. I want to be yours. Forever."

He sealed my vow with a kiss.

And I forgot all about Cassius' words as I fell asleep in his arms, my body facing the fire, the warmth hot on my face as his arms wrapped me up from behind.

I forgot about the flames.

I forgot about it all.

CHAPTER TWENTY-NINE

SERENITY

Darkness.

There was only darkness when I opened my eyes. I pulled myself from Mason's body as a chill shook through me. It wasn't normal for me to feel such extreme temperatures. I frowned and looked down at the table, where a thin area of frost lay. I dipped my fingertip in it and squished the ice between my fingertips.

It melted against my skin immediately.

When I turned around, Mason was still sleeping. A smile crossed his perfect lips as he turned away from me and into the couch.

I shivered again and realized I'd need to light a fire if I had any chance of getting the chill out of my bones. Besides, I didn't want Mason waking up cold.

Did immortals like him, ones with mixed blood, even get cold?

So many questions still bounced around in my head. Mainly, I wondered if he would take his place as king, as the Alpha.

And the other part.

Where I was involved.

My parents.

All of it.

I tried to think of my earliest memory, but it had always been my mother's face as she wept with joy over her new baby.

I'd felt such elation that I'd caused her so much happiness that all I felt was contentment in her arms.

I quickly shook the thought away and added a few stacks of dry firewood, some newspaper, and then lit.

The flare erupted in my face. I jumped back as one flame narrowly missed my cheek and then swirled in front of me again like a whip, out to lash my body with its rage.

I scooted back farther.

The flame only followed.

Until my back was against the couch.

The fire stretched to my face and touched my cheek with a fiery singe. I couldn't look away as the flames danced before me; they shifted into wolves around a campfire, howling at the moon in celebration. Tears stung my eyes as a tall hooded figure approached followed by another and another.

Twelve stood tall with the wolves.

The wolves stared right back in their true form, their eyes

piercing through the darkness as the hooded figures lowered.

I gasped at their jet-black hair and clear blue eyes. They were beautiful, too beautiful to be real. I blinked again as they held their heads high, watching, waiting.

"This…" One of the wolves stepped forward and transformed back into a naked man. "…this is not your realm."

"No…" The voice was musical, yet strong. "…it is not."

The wolf glared. "Then why are you here?"

"What will you do, protector? Kick us out?"

He fisted his hands and waited, his jaw tightening as the wind blew some of his hair across his dirty forehead. He was massive, at least seven feet tall, not someone I would want to fight.

"No. We do not kick out friends, no matter how unwelcome they may be at midnight."

The man's lips twitched.

The wolf sighed. "Well, get on with it Danu. What is it that you need?"

The woman at the man's side stepped forward. "We come to give a warning."

"Lovely." The wolf hung his head. "And what would that be?"

Danu hung her head. "I was bribed. His beauty was unlike anything—"

"That is enough, sister!" the man yelled. "Tell them what you have done."

She lifted her head. "I have birthed a babe."

The wolf let out a gruff howl. "The Creator will punish you."

"The Creator," Danu spat, "already has." She shook her head. "The babe will not stay with me. She will spend her time here, on this realm. One day her blood will run in your kin's veins. I ask only this. Protect her. Protect her from the one who might steal her away. A favor is still owed. He will ask it of you."

The wolf hesitated then spoke. "Who has the babe?"

"She's being shielded under the vampire king's watch. He is to keep her safe in this life. And your son..." She choked out the words. "...your son will do the rest. She knows nothing of her power, of her shifting abilities. She knows nothing of our world, and because of my sin, she will know only loneliness in yours... until him."

"They must mate..." The wolf said it with a shake of his voice. "...musn't they?"

"He will be her protector, and she will be his serenity." Danu's voice cracked. "Vow this to me, wolf! Vow it!"

The Alpha walked over to the flames and held his hand high. Danu followed and pressed a hand across his forearm, and as both of their joined hands hit the first flame, it wrapped around their arms like an embrace, searing the blood oath into their skin. "What is meant for evil will be good," they said in unison.

"Thank you." A single tear slipped off Danu's face, extinguishing the fire.

"Anything... for the goddess of the earth."

The dirt then strained to touch her legs as she walked back toward the group; it swirled around her, beckoned her, wanted nothing but more of the goddess as she stopped and looked up to the sky and whispered. "Guard her well, my creator. Guard her well."

A star twinkled and then fell from the sky.

"The Creator's promise," the Alpha whispered.

"He is fair." Danu nodded. "He is good."

They retreated into the forest and with a flash of light disappeared. I watched the smoke until my eyes hurt then sleepily rubbed them and collapsed back against the couch.

CHAPTER
THIRTY

MASON

I JOLTED AWAKE to see my mate covered in ash from head to
toe, her eyes blinking, but not really seeing. "Serenity?"

She shook her head and then looked at me as if with new
eyes. "Your father, he was very tall?"

"Odd question, but around seven feet. Why?"

"Do you have pictures of him?"

I brushed some ash from her cheek. "Is there a reason
you're asking about my father after having sex? Is this a
vampire thing? You need to know I have good breeding
stock as a wolf. I know I can—"

She smiled and pressed a hand to my face.

I was embarrassed as I felt my chest rise and fall like it was puffing up with each word that fell from my mouth.

"Stop. It's not that."

My frown deepened as she turned her attention to the fire and whispered. "I looked at the flames."

I sat down on the ground and pulled her into my arms. "And what did they tell you?"

She looked down at her dirty hands and shook her head like she was still in disbelief. "What do you know of Danu?"

I jerked at the name.

The very name my father often talked about with affection as if he was close friends with a being so different from ourselves.

I wasn't sure how to respond. Wolves knew all the ancient texts; we knew secrets only The Creator knew. We knew of realms created only for certain purposes. For her to have knowledge of that was unfathomable.

"Please, Mason?"

I nodded and hoped Cassius would put my head on a pike for saying anything. "Danu was one of the twelve goddesses of earth, originally an angel from the Garden of Eden, set to watch humans." I shifted uncomfortably. "After the fall, The Creator had no use for those angels. Creation was finished, and the angels were in a way more powerful than the rest of the heavenliness. It set them apart enough to cause jealousy, and The Creator had already seen so many of his children fall that he did the only thing he knew to do. He sent the chosen to a separate realm to live out their lives. Some even worshipped them as if they are true gods and goddesses. Only twice a year are they able to enter into the human realm, with one job and one job only. To help nurture the earth and keep it whole for the human race.

They are powerful beyond measure, able to destroy with a single word, to create with a flip of their hand. Their beauty knows no bounds, and they are as dangerous as they are good. Nobody has seen a goddess of the earth since—" I swallowed the lump in my throat. "—since my father did."

"I did," she said quickly. "I saw them."

My head swiveled to her. "What now?"

"In the flames." Her voice shook. "I saw them. I saw him — your father. I think..." She pressed an ashy hand to her face. "...I think Danu's my mother." Her expression darkened. "Is that even possible?"

I opened my door to speak, to tell her no, to say she was dreaming. That a goddess wouldn't choose a human mate or an immortal one. They simply did not mate because they were fine within their own angelic state. Perfect, except for one thing.

Missing their purpose in life, which was always to guard the garden.

And when an immortal no longer had a purpose, a part of them died inside. The part meant for something extraordinary suddenly turned ordinary and was always subject to fall just like humans had and the angels before them.

The door slammed, jolting me out of my slack-jawed appearance and my jumbled thoughts and justifications. Alex strolled in with Hope. Ethan and Genesis soon followed with the twins.

Once Genesis placed the twins in a playpen, the rest of the group addressed us, as if they wanted to make sure everyone was safe, that the house was safe before they did anything.

"The deserters are back," Alex announced spreading

his arms wide. "Heard we missed a great party with some Watchers, but I had to keep my mate safe so… we went to a hotel downtown, had the best steak, Mason. Ah, you would have orgasmed on the spot from this—" Alex stopped talking and looked between us. "You guys been rolling around in the ash?"

I put up my hand and looked to Serenity. "Are you sure that's what you saw?"

She nodded. "Positive. Your father, at least I think it was him, made a pact. They talked about you. They talked about us — as if they knew."

Alex raised his hand. "How about you guys fill us in? Because I thought the only remaining drama here was good ol' Mason growing a pair of balls and marching back into his clan and claiming his spot as king."

I growled. As if I needed to think about that, now that I was staring into the eyes of my mate, a would-be goddess, for howling out loud!

She shrugged. "Maybe it was a hallucination. I'm a vampire, clearly a vampire. I crave blood."

Ethan stared at her briefly and then looked to Alex, his expression damning.

Alex let out a long sigh. "You ever heard of a glamour, sweetheart?"

"Of course." She clung to me tighter.

Alex shrugged. "Could be that. I helped do it to Steph. She thought she was a siren for hundreds of years. Nope, all Dark One."

She wasn't there to yell at him.

He snorted. "She wishes she were a siren. We get all the nice tricks."

Hope rolled her eyes.

"How could you tell?" Serenity asked the question I didn't want anyone answering.

But Alex had a ginormous mouth, so he simply said, "Cassius would know. Or any angel for that matter." His smirk grew when he nodded to me and asked, "You dye your hair? She got a little angel fantasy."

"No, you jackass." I threw a pillow at his face. "Apparently, I'm housing a Watcher! But thanks for caring!"

Alex paled. "Seriously?"

"No, I like red and black. They look good with my CLAWS!" I roared. "Yes, so not only do I crave blood like it's my only chance of life, but when I turn into a wolf, I turn white now, and to top it all off, I look like a freaking psychopath!"

"You don't look like a psychopath," Serenity said helpfully, patting my arm as if I was a child.

I hated how it calmed me, her touch, the way her fingers grazed my skin, making my wolf rumble inside with the need to smell her neck, to taste her tongue.

I stood.

Alex backed up.

Ethan put an arm around Genesis and pushed her out of the way.

I rolled my eyes. "I'm not really one of them. I'm me—"

"Just taller," Hope added with a wink.

Alex elbowed her.

Ethan grumbled out, "Insanely strong and angelic-like sure, but it's still you."

"Any more Watcher bodies who need a hand? Because I gotta say I could totally dig a nine pack." Alex patted his stomach and winked.

I was ready to rip his head from his shoulders when

Cassius entered with Stephanie, looking way too pleased to make me comfortable.

Alex coughed and looked away.

Cassius ignored us completely and stared down Serenity. "So now you know."

She nodded. "I guess. I mean, what am I really?"

"You're you," he said vaguely. Not helpfully.

"Is this a glamour?" She pointed to her beautiful body.

I would have been disappointed if it was. I loved her body, loved that it took care of her soul for so many years for me, despite my stubbornness and arrogance.

Cassius jerked his head to me. "Ask Mason."

"Mason isn't an angel," Alex pointed out dumbly.

"He may not be Gadreel in soul, but he has his memories and all the other attributes that made the Watchers special. He would be able to tell."

"I haven't seen anything." I lifted my hands into the air. "Only her."

"Because you only want to see her. You don't want to see beyond what your eyes tell you." Cassius, again with the vagueness.

I scratched my head in frustration then braced Serenity with both hands, looking deep into her swirling eyes.

And. Saw. Nothing.

"Maybe kiss her," Alex joked. "Always works in the fairy tales."

"He's been doing more than kissing her," Ethan said in a hushed tone.

"Could all of you please just—" I took a deep breath and tried to focus on what Cassius said. Her, I need to see beyond what I wanted to see.

What I wanted to see was my mate.

Don't look at her like your mate.

Impossible.

I squeezed my eyes shut then opened them, focusing in on her smooth skin and straight hair. A small movement near her heart caught my eye.

I reached out and touched the ripple in the air.

And every single window in the entire house blew out.

CHAPTER THIRTY-ONE

SERENITY

I FLEW BACK against the wall as pieces of glass filled the air in slow motion, hitting furniture and immortal, not taking any prisoners. I tried reaching for Mason as my back slammed against the wall.

It was useless.

I hit with such force it stole all the breath from my lungs.

I crumbled to the floor and coughed as the glass from the windows made a crashing noise against the ground.

And then seven pairs of eyes were trained on me…

In a mixture of worry.

And awe.

I didn't feel any different.

If anything, I felt like I'd just been run over by a truck; my head hurt, my eyes stung, and my body felt too heavy to stand.

Mason rushed to my side; his shaking hand pushed hair from my face with such reverence that I wanted to weep.

"What?" I croaked out, even my voice sounded different, sharper. "What's wrong?"

Alex peered around Mason and gave me a satisfied smile before saying, "Well, well, well… looks like there's finally someone strong enough to give me a run for my money."

I frowned down at my glowing palms then slid my tongue over my fangs. Thank God, they were still there.

Cassius simply shrugged. "She was born of this earth, fully vampire, fully immortal, half goddess." He stopped and then lowered his voice. "Half Watcher."

I flinched at the word *Watcher*.

And then realized all too soon.

My mate looked just like one.

Did that mean I looked like my mother?

Mason hung his head as he dropped my hand. "You knew?"

Cassius sighed; it was long and drawn out, as if he didn't want to have the conversation. "You're aware that I see all possible futures, but whenever it comes to those closest to me, there is only so much I can see, Mason."

A trickle of blood ran down my lip. Mason reached out and caught it with his hand. "Is this why her blood tastes so good to me? Is she what brings out the vampire?"

I flinched when he said *she*.

As if I wasn't his mate anymore.

As if I was this unreachable being that just happened

to be sitting in front of him and in his house. I still felt that tether of connection between us, but I also felt pain, insecurity. I felt betrayal, and it was all directed at me.

I tried to climb into myself as I hugged my knees to my chest and looked away. When would I ever learn?

I was the problem.

Me.

People always left me.

Should have known. I was a freak.

He would leave too.

Just like them.

"You crave her blood because it is the very blood that keeps you alive, wolf." Cassius said the words with venom, as if he was pissed he even had to utter them. "She is the only reason that Bannick was able to use Gadreel as an anchor to make you what you are today. You want to know why you are powerful? Why you are the true Alpha? Why you are alive and breathing today rather than crippled the way your disease would have left you? Look no further than the sacrifice she made the minute she was brought into this world — and bound, to one such as you."

Mason closed his eyes as the room fell into a tense silence.

And slowly, one by one, people rose and left, not once making eye contact with Mason, but nodding to me, as if I was in the right. And he was in the wrong.

He didn't move.

Finally, I stood, and tried to walk past him.

His hand jerked out and grabbed my wrist. "I was afraid. I didn't mean—"

I pulled away and walked off whispering under my breath. "I'm going to go to sleep."

I could feel the pain in Mason's chest at our separation;

the way his body ached to join with mine was so real that it made me catch my breath as I slowly made my way up the stairs.

I stopped when Hope gave me a look and then pulled me into the bathroom and shut the door behind her.

"He was wrong," she said in a small voice, "to react that way, but he's wolf. One thing you need to know about wolves is they react. It's what they were born to do, to react, to heal, and above all else to protect their clans."

"What about their mates?" I suddenly jerked up my chin. "Doesn't it matter who I am?"

Her brown eyes softened. "It does when he has to face his family again, a family he left a long time ago — a clan all but abandoned. He is the rightful king. How do you think they will react to his return? With the way he looks? With the way you look? Bad enough that he mated a vampire."

I tried not to be offended.

"What's worse… you have goddess blood mixed in your veins, and people tend to be fearful of what they don't understand. Who's to say you don't destroy them all?"

I scoffed. "I would never do that! I don't even have any power."

Her eyebrows shot up. "Maybe tell that to all the windows Ethan's going to have to replace." She touched my arm softly, "Look, I'm not giving him a free pass. All men are assholes — we can agree on that — but he already feels like the cards are stacked against him, and this was a surprising blow to an already full deck, alright? Don't doubt his feelings for you. This is more about him, about his place, and let's be honest, had he done the right thing all that time ago, this wouldn't even be a big deal."

I gave her a look.

She smirked. "Okay, so it would be a big deal but not like… apocalyptic or world-ending."

My eyes widened. "It's not that bad."

"To the true Alpha, it will feel that way. There are certain—" She stopped as if she wasn't sure she should say it. After glancing at the door, she lowered her voice. "—there are certain rituals you will need to take part in once he takes his rightful place, certain things you'll see and…" She licked her lips. "…do."

I rubbed my arms as the sound of footsteps neared the bathroom door. Hope gave me a nod before going to it and pulling it open. Alex had his hand up ready to knock. He was shirtless, his low-slung leather pants hung so painfully past what was appropriate that I had to look in his eyes. And something about his eyes always made me feel like he was… probing.

I didn't like it.

He smirked as if he he knew it and then kissed Hope on the cheek, "Ready for our shower?"

"I think that's my cue." I felt my cheeks heat as I pushed past both of them and walked down the hall.

Did I go to Masons room?

Or the room I'd been staying in?

Awkward didn't even begin to cover it.

I'd never felt so wrongfully out of place, my heart knew which direction to walk in, my soul screamed, my blood pounded against my flesh, and yet my mind told me that I should sleep it off — alone, give him space.

Give us space.

So much had happened in the span of forty-eight hours.

Slowly, I walked back to the room that I'd been staying with and pulled off my shoes and clothes, with each garment

I peeled away, I felt more and more distance stretch between me and Mason, until my chest ached so much I couldn't stop the tears from falling down my cheeks.

I didn't ask to be born this way.

I didn't ask to live a life of complete isolation and loneliness.

I curled into a ball and started to drift to sleep when the door to my room opened, footsteps sounded, the bed creaked, and then a warm body was lying down next to mine, its muscular form too great to ignore as I stilled next to him.

"Never again," Mason whispered in my ear. "Never walk away from me again without talking to me first. I'm your mate, not Hope, not Alex, not Ethan, not Cassius—" He growled in the back of his throat. "You. Are. Mine." His teeth grazed the edge of my ear, and then he sighed, his head pressed against my neck. "I can be an ass."

I didn't move. I was afraid he'd see the tear-stained sheets or the runny nose that refused to go away even though I had stupid goddess blood in my veins.

"I'm sorry." Mason tried again. "Hurting you, making you feel anything other than the most important person in my existence is inexcusable."

I nodded as he tugged the sheet away and very slowly tilted my head toward him.

Icy blue eyes locked with mine as he whispered, "I'm responsible for these." He gently ran his tongue up my neck as a tear collided with him, over and over again. He pressed his tongue, his mouth to the wet salty spots and then hesitated. His eyes held a sadness I only knew because of the quivering of the tether between us, as if his heart was skipping beats because it wasn't strong enough to go on.

"What's wrong?" I whispered, afraid that it was me. That

I was the wrong in his life.

He gave his head a shake, the dark pieces of hair falling against my face, I wound them up in my fingers and flinched when the red pieces touched my skin and caused an electric jolt to shoot through my system.

His expression was grave. "The red represents the sin. Whenever another immortal touches it, it's a reminder."

"A reminder?" I whispered.

His forehead touched mine. "Not to listen to our feelings, but to listen to the truth."

"What's truth?" Frustration welled up within me. "I feel like my entire life I've been living a lie, as cliché as that sounds, and now I'm supposed to blindly trust. Why? Give me one reason. Why?"

"Because…" It was as if a switch of light turned on Mason's face as he almost glimmered before me. "The Creator is good, and he allows us… the great privilege… of a choice."

Instantly ashamed, I looked away. "Would you have chosen this though? This life? You were sick as a boy. That's why they gave you my blood, angel blood. Would you have chosen differently, Mason? Given your…" I knew it was a touchy subject, but I was his mate. If we couldn't talk about it, then we couldn't be together. "…given your first mate dying? The life of solitude you lived?"

"Listen—" Mason almost growled the word out., "—very carefully," He cupped my face with both hands, the warmth of his palms seeping into my skin. "There is nothing I would do different. There is no better life in existence than life in your arms, than life…" He pressed a hot palm to my chest. "…shared with this heart."

I didn't realize I was crying until his tongue was on my

cheek again.

And then the rest of my clothes were discarded as his tongue sought every other pleasure it could find, while I bucked beneath each touch like he was searing me, marking me more and more, and when he bit into my thigh, all I saw was light, goodness...

Us.

The tether between us pulled tight, strengthened.

"You are my mate, made for me, since the beginning."

"Yes," I agreed as our bodies moved together, as he took me on another wave of pleasure, as I felt his thickness inside of me, reminding me, that I wasn't alone anymore.

That I had a partner.

That I wasn't abandoned.

Betrayed.

I was his.

I was an *us*.

I soared with him to higher heights and swore then and there that I would die to protect the wolf I married. I would die to protect the heart he carried inside his chest, the one that pumped so valiantly for his people, for me, for humans.

I would die.

With no regrets.

And I fell asleep, with a smile on my lips.

CHAPTER THIRTY-TWO

MASON

IT WAS TIME.

I felt it in my bones like I had when I was a lad.

The same hunger that forced me to crawl on my hands and knees to the window and beg The Creator to make me the Great Wolf.

He'd granted my wish.

It had dire consequences.

I still had no idea what my mate was capable of, and yet, I knew it would be all right. I just didn't know how. I trusted the fact that I had the knowledge of the stars in my make-up — the way that Gadreel had left it. I just wished I knew how to access all the information in a way that would help me regain the trust and reverence of my people.

I knew I had my warriors.

But I did not have the rest of the people.

The minute I turned against my true nature was the minute they'd called me weak. It had nearly killed me.

To call a wolf weak, to hear it throughout the world in harsh whispers and discontent, as if I was a poison set about the wolf race, to end them all…

It had shaken my already broken heart and nearly left me for dead.

Until Cassius.

Ethan.

Stephanie.

Begrudgingly, I even admitted Alex's sarcasm turned my focus to wanting to murder him more than the people who doubted my strength, my ability to be the Great Wolf, the Alpha.

I rolled to my side and watched her sleep.

My mate.

My goddess.

My vampire.

What beautiful blood she had running through her veins. What an impossible task we had set before us.

My mind — my entire body — begged me to default, to put on my torn jeans, to grab my flip-flops from the Goodwill, and put my hair in a ponytail. To march downstairs and hunt some berries, to suffer a crunchy pinecone-filled breakfast.

My body wanted me to be punished.

My soul demanded it.

My mind told me I was no longer worthy.

But my blood — her blood — whispered, *"You are."*

And for the first time in my existence, I chose to believe something other than the negative thoughts in my own brain.

I trusted the blood.

I trusted her.

I closed my eyes. This was so different, living a life of depravity made me feel — better. Any wolf would see me and see the suffering. The judgement had never been narcissism, only pity for my state.

It had helped me stay in that condition, their pity.

And so I'd stayed.

Warriors had stopped begging my return.

And the whispers stopped.

And I was lost.

Because when you lose your purpose, you lose your very soul.

Mine had not been returned to me, until I faced what I was, what I was becoming with her.

I pushed the jet-black hair from her perfect face. She was even pretty when she slept, her earth-toned skin, the kind formed by the hands of The Creator alone shone in all its glory. It's dizzying pieces of onyx twinkled with delight.

Maybe they'd be so distracted by her beauty they would not remember the old tales.

But I knew some of them were still alive. Some of them would know.

One of them for sure.

My father.

CHAPTER THIRTY-THREE

SERENITY

I jolted awake, a deep apprehension and sadness assaulting me. I turned on my side as Mason slowly put his feet over the edge of the bed and hung his head in his hands, his angel-like hair falling down his muscular back.

I wanted to make it better.

Had to.

"Mason." I touched his shoulder.

His hand connected with mine; he squeezed so tight my fingers went white before I scooted closer to him and pressed my breasts up against his back. "Fifteen more minutes."

"Fifteen more minutes will nae change it."

"No," I said softly, "but it might take some of your stress away."

He was wound up so tense I wasn't even sure a practiced masseuse could get the knots out. I slowly kneaded his back and then wrapped my body around his, straddling his naked lap with extreme purpose as he lifted his parted lips to mine. "You mean to seduce me?"

I moved against him then whispered, "I think I already did."

He cupped my ass and positioned himself at my entrance. "You sure about that?"

I looked down. "Yeah, Mason, I'm pretty sure."

He growled in response as he thrust into me. Had he not been hanging onto my body I would have fallen backward off the bed and cracked my head. With each drive, I felt his stress lighten, so much that, when his body strained taut, I said with a firm voice, "Give it to me."

He hesitated, his eyes unfocused.

"Or at least share it with your mate, Mason. Let me help."

"It's my cross to bear."

"Now…" I took control, slowing his rhythm down as I pressed a kiss to his mouth. "…it's ours."

"Aye."

I didn't comment on the sudden Scottish brogue or the fact that he didn't seem to recognize the fact that he was under so much stress that he'd reverted back to what was natural.

"Ours," I repeated.

"Forever." His gravelly promise against my tongue.

CHAPTER
THIRTY-FOUR

MASON

She fell asleep across my chest, this strange, beautiful creature that I knew I didn't deserve, that I hadn't even wanted, but would die to keep, to protect.

My gut clenched as my heart sank.

What if?

That's all I had.

What if?

I couldn't.

I wouldn't go through it again.

Losing anyone in my life that meant the world, meant my existence, and in such a short time, everything pointed to her, to her essence, to the make of who she was, and I couldn't separate the fact that I needed to be Alpha, needed to be Wolf King in order to unite us with the fact that I had to do it with her by my side.

My only weakness.

Vulnerability.

My greatest and most valuable risk.

Her lips were red then, like she'd just chewed her lower lip, thinking of the way I'd done the same a few minutes before, and I selfishly wondered if she thought of me, of the way I tasted her, of the way I spread her legs wide and licked her core like she was my own personal meal.

Of the way I pierced her skin.

The blood trickling into my mouth.

The way I owned her.

Marked her.

I gripped her hips again as she moaned and knew I would never linger when it came to claiming her, to wanting her, because she was in my blood, my soul. I just had to know she would be safe.

She had to be safe.

Every single old fear I'd ever harbored floated to the surface in a wave of anxiety that crushed my spirit, my soul.

I kissed her brow and quietly got up and went downstairs to think.

I had to be away from her because with her, all I saw was her.

By the time I made it into the living room I knew my thoughts were not private, that Cassius knew my fear. He was sitting by the fire looking like he had a lot on his mind, on his soul, the way mine was heavy.

"You're up late." I took a seat.

Without flinching, he said, "I don't sleep much anymore." His eyes were grave as he looked at me and then back at the fire. "Fear is not welcome here."

I hung my head. "I haven't known true fear until this moment in time."

"Fear will only breed hate," he said gravely.

"Hate?" I paced in front of him. "I don't understand."

He stood, and his eyes flashed white before he said quickly, "Not now you don't, but you will."

He disappeared in a flash of light, and I was left in front of the crackling fire place wondering if everything would ever feel safe again.

If anything would feel normal.

Or if I was cursed to feel the weight of the universe on my shoulders right along with its secrets.

I never understood the sheer horror at knowing the secrets around me, the way the earth moaned and ached for the angels to return home almost as much as they themselves ached.

My chest was in a constant state of pain, and I now knew why.

It was the same aching pain the Watchers felt on a daily basis.

Passed down to me.

It wasn't just physical pain.

I knew what that felt like.

No, this was emotional turmoil that wouldn't go away; it was the deepest separation I'd ever experienced. It only faded away when I was with Serenity, when I was united with love.

When I feared, it pierced my heart.

I looked into the flames as dawning realization shook me to my core. The Watchers were not tempted to do evil in order to regain the attention of The Creator. No, it was much worse than that.

They'd been walking around for millennia with a broken heart.

The thought haunted me as I took a seat, and when Serenity joined me hours later, laying her head against my chest, and peppered kisses down my skin, when I felt peace in her arms, I knew.

The war wasn't over.

It had only just begun.

CHAPTER
THIRTY-FIVE

SERENITY

"It's only a few days." Mason took one look at my bag and smirked, the corners of his eyes crinkling as he watched me with interest.

"What?" I looked down at the duffle bag Hope had given me that morning. "This isn't mine."

"It has your name on the tag." He grinned wider.

I huffed out a breath. "Hope gave it to me."

"Likely story." Aggravating wolf! "That's enough clothes for a few weeks."

"Well I would have gone back to my apartment, but somebody wouldn't let me." I gave him a challenging glare.

His smile fell. "My job is to protect you. I still don't know who's after you. If they can track you because you return, no, you won't be seeing your apartment anytime soon. Everything you need is here."

I crossed my arms. "I can't just hide forever."

"We're not hiding." His jaw flinched. "There's a war, Serenity, and I can't focus on leading my people, on even meeting with them, if I think for one second you aren't safe."

His eyes blazed blue as his chest rose and fell. Even now, I wondered if he realized that his right hand was more claw than man, that the heat emitting from him was anything but normal, but he didn't seem to notice. His eyes had laser-like focus, and it was all on me.

I nodded. "You're right. I'm sorry."

"Damn it." He turned around as if he was frustrated then stomped up to me and slammed me against the wall, his hands cupping my head so I didn't get hurt. "I don't want you to be sorry. I don't want to order you around. I just—" Pain laced his eyes as he searched my face. "—I will not lose you."

He didn't even say *can*, as if it was an option.

It was a vow. An oath.

"I won't." He devoured my mouth, sucking the life out of my body as his hands palmed my ass, one talon digging a bit into my flesh. "I won't." He growled again against my mouth.

I pulled back. "I promise, Mason."

He still looked worried as I slid down the wall out of his arms then side-stepped him and grabbed my bag. "So how do we do this?"

"What?'" His confused expression was priceless.

"This." I waved my hands around "Does Cassius just fly

us over there?"

He barked out a laugh. "Well typically, we take a plane, but maybe Cassius wouldn't mind a little transport…"

"Drop dead," came Cassius' voice, and then he was in the room, arms crossed, expression haunted. "First class not good enough for you? Private plane? Name it, and I'll see it done."

My eyes widened with each word that came out.

Mason just shrugged. "She wants to fly."

I grinned at the idea.

"I'm not flying you to Scotland." Cassius rolled his eyes, looking more human than I'd seen him in weeks. His dark hair went white as he sighed and opened up his arms as wings appeared, and then he muttered out a "Damn wolf…" before nodding to me and saying, "Touch a feather."

"Really?" I tried to play it cool, but I'd been wanting to touch his feathers, to feel the texture between my fingers for days. "Any feather?"

"Or all of them." Cassius grinned.

Mason growled like there was something I didn't know about touching the feathers.

I took a step forward and reached out to one of the plumes that curved down the wing; it shuddered under my grasp then wrapped its velvety tentacles around my finger and pulsed with my heart. It was warm. It felt… like heaven, like I never wanted to let go.

"She's going to ask to touch them all the time now," Mason grumbled.

"She's very gentle." Cassius winked at me. I knew he was trying to make Mason irritated, which proved true when Mason gripped one of the feathers with one hand and smacked Cassius with the other.

I gasped.

Was that allowed?

Hitting an archangel?

Hitting Cassius? Basically, the king of the entire immortal race?

Cassius simply smirked and then nodded. "Now. That's settled. Let's go."

"Wait!" I said in a panicked voice. "Do I have to do anything?"

Both of them stared at me like I was an idiot.

I glared. "You know, like hold my breath... close my eyes..."

"It will be seconds," Cassius said gently, "Just enjoy the ride." He looked over to Mason and grinned widely. "I know I will."

"That's enough." Mason growled as Cassius' laughter filled the room, his eyes completely white as his wings curved around us.

And just like that.

I was weightless.

CHAPTER
THIRTY-SIX

MASON

ALL TOO SOON, we were in Edinburgh near the castle. Cassius landed between one of the least popular closes of the Royal Mile. My blood boiled as memories haunted me, of the sick that used to roam the streets, the plague that went underground for so long, the people living on top of people. The sheer disgust of the city, the rank disease that ran through it, years of no sunlight for some humans only to die in the dark alone without ever feeling the sun's heat on their faces.

I turned my head to Serenity.

She saw the city with eyes that were new. Like a tourist,

it seemed she wanted to take everything in, bad enough that the minute her eyes landed on a tartan, she started moving.

I jerked her backward and shook my head.

Cassius' wings were tucked away as the three of us walked into the sunlight in the street.

Immediately, a few locals looked our way.

I tried to stay calm.

Tried and failed, as the few that saw me and Cassius became many. There was a reason immortals stayed in the States, a corrupt country with a selfish race of people who'd rather spend time on social media than look at the world around them.

They were obsessed with money, fame, themselves.

Scotland had its faults. It also had its stories.

Namely, its legends.

And as I walked toward the castle, a tourist trap if I'd ever seen one, hand-in-hand with Serenity, Cassius nodded to people who passed.

And I knew.

My time was up.

Maybe it had been up all this time.

All the secrets. All the loneliness. All the shame that had welled up within me was bursting free with every step I took toward my destiny with my mate at my side.

The final puzzle piece.

The last of the mated immortals, taking my rightful place that I'd ignored for centuries.

Because it hurt too deeply.

But now... now I had Serenity.

I had peace. I clung to the peace as hard as I could. And when I felt like I couldn't take another step, I did.

More and more locals poured out of the shops. Their

minds were abuzz with the phrase, *"It has begun."*

Cassius kept his gaze focused ahead.

I followed and then jolted to a stop when I heard someone utter, "The Great Wolf has returned."

Serenity gasped next to me.

Someone stood taller from the crowd; he had dark brown hair and jet-black eyes. I recognized him immediately.

And my heart cracked inside its chest as my brother very slowly weaved his way toward me and stopped.

I was a foot taller than he.

Stronger.

Different... and yet the same.

I had the pieces of red in my hair that hadn't been there before, but all he seemed to focus on was my eyes.

"Why've ye returned?"

"To take my place." I said it with such finality, and he flinched. Fear laced his eyes as he looked from me to Serenity.

"And the woman?"

"My mate." I growled.

A few people gasped around us.

I turned away and kept walking.

He called for me.

And I ignored him.

He was younger, born a hundred years after me to my father's new wife after the death of my mother. My father had no longer wanted me, not cared for me. Even the times Cassius brought me back to visit, I'd been unwanted, until the day I took my place and then lost my mate.

Lost it all.

My mind, my sanity...

And now... returned.

"Do not let your fear turn to hate," Cassius whispered as

we walked to the front of the castle gate.

A few men stood watch as they always did against the outside world or a drunk wandering tourist who went into the wrong tunnel at the precise right time.

I watched and waited as slowly the five men came forward and addressed us with a single nod of their heads.

I let out a breath, and we followed them south around the castle and then down a flight of stairs into a tunnel that had a giant sign in front of it. *DANGER Do Not Enter.*

We walked through.

The tunnel continued on for a mile before we descended the stairs and were brought into the first throne room.

"Mason," Serenity said at my side, "why are we in a castle underneath a castle?"

I shook my head then hung it in shame.

"Royalty," Cassius answered for me. "I thought you knew he was a king?"

"I did," she said quickly. "I just thought that was a fancy word for Alpha or that he was King of the Wolves."

"Nae…" A warrior stepped forward. "He is King of the Land."

"Land," Serenity repeated.

And Cassius whispered, "Earth."

CHAPTER THIRTY-SEVEN

MASON

I closed my eyes as Serenity's breath hitched beside me, finally cluing in to how important my job had been — and how severe my absence had hit my clan. And noat just my clan, but every warrior guarding the earth, spread around the world.

I didn't recognize the warrior in front of me.

He stared me down for a few brief seconds before muttering, "He's nae gonna wanna see ya."

"He," I stated boldly, "doesn't get say, now does he?"

Cassius smirked next to me.

"And who are ye?" He gave Cassius a disgusted look.

Cassius' eyes flashed white before his wings spread out behind his back. With a little shrug, he said, "Oh, nobody."

The warrior stumbled back and made a cross over his heart while I tried to keep from laughing.

The wolves had always believed that when an angel visited, it only meant death, and maybe this time that was true, because the only way I was going to be able to claim my right...

To lead my people...

Was to kill the one I'd left in charge.

My own flesh and blood.

My father.

CHAPTER
THIRTY-EIGHT

SERENITY

I WAS DUMBFOUNDED.

Stunned.

We walked hand in hand down black marble stairs as the room opened up into a larger room where an actual throne made out of black marble sat in the middle of the floor. The air smelled like dirt and life. I shivered as Mason pulled me closer.

For some reason, I'd been thinking that we were going to the castle I'd seen in the vision, or maybe to a small village.

Never in my wildest imagination had I thought we would be stepping into pure royalty.

Wolf guards lined the walls as we made our descent, and with each step we took, they bowed out of respect for who Mason was.

How was it possible that I'd had it so wrong? That any immortal was this clueless to the power the wolves held, the responsibility.

Suddenly my chest hurt, because if Mason turned away from this— His grief... it must have been so great, life-altering, destroying...

To walk away from everything.

And have nothing. On purpose.

Because of a choice.

A broken heart.

"I dinna like that face," Mason whispered in my ear, his Scottish burr tickling my skin. I wanted to point out how he sounded more at home and looked it in this place, but I didn't want to scare him off before he had to do what he had to do.

And because he still left me in the dark and closed that tether between us out of respect, I let him lead me without knowing exactly what we were walking into.

The throne came closer into our view. It stretched from floor to ceiling, glistening with power, glory, as if it had been dropped from the heavens itself.

Cassius leaned over and whispered, "A gift from The Creator, for the protector of the very earth he created. It was formed out of the rock, and it remains without blemish to honor him until the heavens meet the earth again."

I gulped.

More warriors gathered around us, their golden shields held by their feet, spears in their right hands, and masks in the shape of wolves over their human faces.

The sound of thunder rolled through the room.

And then, someone walked from behind the throne and sat.

The man from my vision. The man with dark hair and dark eyes.

At least seven feet tall with muscles surrounding his body.

He was wearing the same armor as the guards, only he had no mask. His expression was more of an angry grimace, as if he was just waiting for the perfect time to attack.

His eyes took in Mason with disdain and then turned to me.

I cringed as they moved over my body with distaste and then flickered away. "You dare bring an abomination into this court?"

"I dare." Mason growled loudly. "I am the rightful king." Whisperings commenced, "I once gave you the throne, and I'm here to take it back."

"Kill the woman, and I'll allow it."

"You allow nothing, old man." Mason's teeth clenched. "Speak of my mate again like that, and I'll rip your head from your body."

His father sighed and then grinned. "You've always been so serious... As long as she means us no harm, she can stay."

"Harm?" I said aloud. "I'm his mate. All I want is his happiness."

"You're nae welcome to speak!" He spat.

I jerked back against Mason.

He took a step forward, fists clenched.

"Enough," Cassius said in a bored tone. "I think this is a conversation that should be held... in private."

Mason's father nodded and moved his hand. Suddenly warriors flanked us on every side, and we were escorted behind the throne into a smaller room with a long black marble table and leather chairs. Flat-screen TVs made a banner around the room. Different cameras played areas of the castle and what appeared to be different places around the world.

Children played on some of the screens; others showed remote villages, a few smaller castles.

And then there was one camera set on a forest.

I frowned and took a step closer.

I remembered the vision from earlier. The forest that the goddess had walked out of.

My mother?

The one who had given me life?

A pang I didn't know possible split my chest in two as I yearned for someone — anyone — to walk out of the trees.

To want me.

To claim me.

And then I remembered I had Mason.

He was all I would ever need.

I glanced back at him and smiled, just as another door opened and the man from the street waltzed in.

He stopped right in front of Mason then pulled him in for a huge hug. He slapped his back multiple times before releasing him. The man had light brown eyes and golden hair that was pulled back into a low ponytail.

I'd always thought men with long hair looked ridiculous.

But the way Mason rocked his shaggy locks…

The way it felt to tug his hair when he pressed into me…

I shivered a bit as Mason growled under his breath next to me, as if I needed to stop distracting him from his purpose.

Cassius gave me a small smile before Mason's father cleared his threat and said, "Shall we begin?"

"There is nothing to say that hasn't already been said." Mason shrugged, his voice cool. "I'm here to lead my people. You are no longer needed."

Mason's father slammed his hands onto the table as he looked between his son and me. "And what of her? Do you truly think your people will accept anything other than a human mate? One chosen for you so you can have children?"

I frowned. "Who says I can't?"

"Lass—" Mason's brother gave his head a small shake.

Cassius grinned as if it was the best day of his life.

"What?" I crossed my arms. "I'm not just a vampire—"

Mason hissed out a curse.

"Abomination!" his father yelled. "She is both vampire and goddess. She cannot rule by your side. It is forbidden." Something flashed in his eyes before he turned and stomped off.

Mason's brother sighed and held out his hand to me. I took it while he kissed the inside of my wrist. "Mother would have loved you."

Mason tensed.

"When did she die?"

He gave me a funny look, "She dinna—" He hung his head. "—she—"

"Tell him." Cassius leveled Mason's brother with a glare. "Tell him, Tarick."

Tarick went completely pale.

Mason frowned. "Tell me what?"

Tarick collapsed into one of the chairs and leaned over the large marble table. "She dinna get murdered, Mason." His expression was bleak. "She took her own life essence when father pushed you to mate, to become king. His intentions... they were not in the right place, and she knew it."

"What do you mean?"

Tarick cursed under his breath. "He was trying to prevent you… from finding… her."

All eyes fell to me.

And suddenly, I was sick all over again.

More pieces of the puzzle came together in a wave of memories, in the dreams I'd had searching for my wolf.

In the dreams every year that had haunted me.

Until this year.

When I'd finally found him.

CHAPTER
THIRTY-NINE

MASON

I ALMOST COLLAPSED against the wall. "No." I gave my head a shake, hoping to get the betrayal out of my skin. It was a poison. My own family? "Why would he do that? Why would she let him?"

Cassius stood to his full height. "When one makes a deal with an angel... when one sells his soul... blood must be spilled. A life for a life. When Bannick saved you, fused your blood with Serenity, he bonded your lives together. Together you'd have strength beyond your wildest imaginations. Apart, you would always thirst, always yearn for more. You would experience an emptiness in your soul." Cassius nodded. "I finally understand. I can finally see." His eyes were white as he looked to Mason and whispered, "You must fight."

He disappeared in a flash of light, much the same way he came.

Tarick's mouth dropped open. "He always do that?"

"Unfortunately." I licked my lips and tried to think. "Tarick, how many of the men are loyal to me?"

He braced himself with the chair. I hadn't noticed how much he'd matured and grown, from this awkward wolf to warrior himself, from his wise tawny brown eyes to the way he braced himself around me, as if he was ready to do whatever it took to draw blood on my behalf. Every sinew of muscle flexed with the ability to kill, to maim effortlessly.

His jaw clenched. "All of them."

"Tarick..." My voice held warning. "I won't punish them if they side with my father. I abandoned our people, but I need them united now. The Watchers—"

"So it's true?" His eyes lit up with shock. "Is that why your hair has those funny red streaks? Never seen sooch colors on a wolf."

"Long story," I mumbled, sharing a cautious look with Serenity. She had questions, and I had no answers. And I was sick with the thought that all of my life I had never questioned those around me, questioned authority, or even questioned the mating process. I'd done my duty blindly.

And stupidly.

I had not been fit to rule then.

I hoped to The Creator I would be fit to rule now.

"Come." Tarick slapped me on the back. "You'll want to get cleaned up for dinner."

He led us down a black marble hallway. The walls were lit with torches while lights shone overhead. Edinburgh Castle had been built to honor the wolves, but after years passed, it had turned into something for humans.

We'd allowed them their separate space.

Taking jobs as warriors and protecting them as was our duty for the earth, but that didn't mean we didn't try to grasp modern technology.

I gripped Serenity's hand. "The last time I walked these halls there wasn't even electricity."

"Grumpy old wolf," she teased under her breath.

My throat caught on a laugh as I pulled her closer. We rounded the corner to the family suites, each of them over three-thousand-square feet.

The door to mine was locked shut.

The picture of my wolf shone across the wood grain. I ran my hand over it and shuddered at the power that sizzled beneath my fingertips.

"Dinners' at six," Tarick said and then seemed to want to say more; instead, he slapped me on the back again and walked off.

Serenity gaped when I thrust open the doors. A massive four-poster bed was pushed against the east wall. A large in-ground tub took up half the space in the middle of the bathroom, and petals swirled around the jets. There were no windows, but we were used to living within the earth. We didn't need to see outside of the dirt to know its secrets. There wasn't any need to see the sky when creation, when the dirt itself, covered us in its splendor.

Serenity gasped out. "It's beautiful."

"It was mine. Or it *is* mine."

She walked over to the bed and stared. "Did she share this bed with you?"

I'd known the question was coming. It hadn't made me

any more prepared. "No."

Her shoulders sagged as she leaned back against me. "Good."

"Jealous?" I nipped her ear. How had I ever thought I could survive without a partner? Without love?

She turned in my arms so fast I almost stumbled backward. Her green eyes flashed with hunger, and they pierced through me to my soul. "You're mine."

I leaned down and took her lower lip, squeezing it between my teeth before whispering, "Then claim me."

Within seconds, her clothes were discarded. I didn't paid attention to where they went. All I knew was that my mate, my true mate, the one meant for me from the beginning of time, was standing in my room naked.

I worshipped her mouth while I kicked down my jeans, my need so strong that my release was already pulsing. Our tongues twisted while her fingers scratched my head, digging, tugging. I pressed her onto the bed, the one I swore I'd never return to, just like that damn room.

I'd thought it was all evidence of what I was no longer worthy of.

But she made it worth it. Made me feel like I had the strength.

There was no insecurity in her arms, and when she pressed me against the wall with her lithe body, there was no doubt in my mind, no fear that I would hurt her or that she would call me heavy.

Or a brute.

No, if anything, my mate wanted me hard against her; she wanted her nails scraping down my back as I licked pleasure through her skin, as I laved up the taste of her skin and spread it across my tongue.

My eyes rolled back when she gripped me in her hand, her touch firm, then soft.

I grabbed her wrist and tugged her into my arms, turning her back against the same dirt wall, and we joined together. As we mated in the very castle where years ago I'd been born.

The dirt around us began to shake.

I clung to her body as we broke apart.

Tiny diamond-like pieces of dirt began to break away from the walls. It twirled in the air and then surrounded us in a circle of light and dark.

Warmth spread through my chest as her eyes flashed green like the grass, blue like the sky, then brown like the earth surrounding us.

The very dirt around us reflected in her eyes with wonder.

A music so old, so beautiful filled the room, and she kissed me again.

The pounding on the door didn't stop us.

The yells only encouraged me to keep claiming her.

And when I could no longer stand the pulsing need clawing at me, ripping me from the inside out, I took her one more time and marked her as mine with one last bite to her neck.

She cried out, while I felt my body surge with power.

And then the dirt fell around us, creating more of a mess than I'd seen in years of being in my room.

"What was that?" Her chest heaved as I dropped her back to her feet.

"The earth approves," I whispered, kissing her gruffly across the mouth again before stalking naked toward the door.

I jerked it open and eyed my brother, ready to wipe the smirk right off his face.

"So…" He bit down on his lip like he was having trouble not laughing out loud. "…you must be quite the lover if you create earthquakes with your giant co—"

"Enough." I cut him off, knowing exactly what he'd been about to say.

He took a step back, "Dinner's ready. I'm sure after that you're… ravenous."

I growled.

"Remember to wear pants, brother. Father is niver forgiving."

I rolled my eyes and slammed the door in his face then turned to see Serenity's hair. She looked thoroughly loved.

"Is dinner formal?"

She started digging through her bags, her naked ass begging me to grab, to claim again and again until I needed rest, until my eyes closed on themselves as I pulsed inside her body.

"Mason?"

I gulped guiltily. "Yes?"

"Stop staring at me and help!" she said frantically. "I don't think I made the best first impression I want to look nice."

"You always look nice," I said truthfully. "And wear the red."

"The red dress?"

"He hates red."

"Then I should wear black."

"Nae…" I smiled. "…red is a symbol of power. Wolves aren't allowed to wear it. We are to be humble even in our ruling of the earth itself. But you're no wolf. You're more, and it's about time he recognized the power you have."

Tears filled her eyes. "I'm still part vampire—"

I swallowed her protest with a kiss. "That you are." I

nodded. "But your blood sings with the earth, I can feel it pulse beneath my fingertips, dancing, singing the song from the earth to the heavens. Give it some time, and maybe you'll be singing to the moon as well."

Tears filled her eyes as she grabbed my hand and kissed the back of it. "I would love that... my king."

Desire so intense attacked me. I pushed her back against the bed, spreading her legs wide. "We can be late."

"You just said—"

"I'm an idiot." I growled, devouring her next protest. "And I will be king if only so I can be late to my own damn table..." I lowered my head. "...and feast on my mate instead."

CHAPTER FORTY

SERENITY

I wore the red.

My legs trembled with nerves as we made our way down a long pathway that at one point broke out so that there were stars overhead. The glass plane over our heads was thick enough that I assumed nobody could see through. The sky was beautiful though.

We walked for what felt like miles.

My feet started to ache.

And then we were in another building. When I turned back and looked through the windows, the castle was in the distance. So, we really had walked a mile or so.

The building appeared old on the outside. But on the inside, there were immaculate riches I could have never comprehended in my long life.

Chandeliers hung down the middle of the room. A roaring fireplace was at the end of the long table for a king.

And Mason's father stood, wearing a black suit and tie as he eyed Mason with fury that even I could sense.

More warriors stood watching, their eyes straight ahead, their shields in place, their armor shining with pride and the insignia of a wolf on their chests.

I wondered if the wolf was Mason.

Or his father.

Or maybe it was someone else.

A few beautiful women were lined up near more men who had different patches and awards on their jackets.

It was this strange alternate reality that I assumed had its own government. It finally made sense why Mason was so important. Why we needed him.

Why the Watchers wanted him too.

He was desired by every world but his own.

And it made me so sad that I couldn't even think about it without my chest hurting, because I knew that pain. I knew it well.

Feeling so out of place.

The feeling of never quite belonging to the place where you were born To parents who never truly wanted you for you.

And just like that, the loss of my own parents washed over me again.

They had been my all.

And they hadn't even told me the truth in their deaths.

I choked back the giant ball in my throat that demanded

I burst into tears and kept walking.

Mason held my hand tightly.

There was a large crack like the sky had opened, and Cassius appeared, dressed in a tux with Stephanie by his side.

Followed by Alex and Hope.

And Ethan and Genesis, sans their twins.

I exhaled a sigh of relief when I saw them — my friends — my new family, here at Mason's side.

His hold on my hand relaxed as Cassius walked up to us and very slowly eyed the room around him. Then with a small smile on his lips, fell to one knee and hung his head.

The room erupted into gasps and wonder as Mason stilled next to me. "Cassius..."

"Bless me," Cassius said. "It is what the King of the Earth does to the King of the Immortals. Is it not?"

I felt the rage of his father.

The rage of others as well.

This was not how things were done. I knew that and was sure the rest of the immortal council did as well as the men all very slowly — Alex included, even though he was smirking the whole time — fell down to one knee and waited.

Mason held out his hand. "It has been a long time. The power has not been transferred..."

"The power has never left," Cassius whispered under his breath.

Mason's eyes widened as he held his hand over Cassius' head, and very slowly, pieces of diamond-like dirt fell from his palm over Cassius like a small rain. And when Cassius lifted his head, the pieces of dirt melted against his skin and twinkled so brightly I almost had to look away.

He stood.

The council followed.

And I attempted to close my mouth.

"Now," Cassius turned to everyone and leveled Mason's father with a glare. "Since that's done, I'd like to vote."

"Vote?" I hissed under my breath.

Mason paled. "Cassius—"

Cassius wouldn't relent. "As King of the Immortals, the archangel to the humans and heavens, keeper of secrets and rightful king of this world until it burns into the next, I demand a vote."

"Nae." Tarik's eyes glistened with barely restrained hatred as he looked from his father back to Mason. "I demand a fight."

The room erupted in outcries.

Cassius nodded to Tarik.

"Can he do that?" I looked up to Mason.

He swallowed very slowly and looked down at me, tilting my chin to his face. "He can, and he did. A fight will be the only way to take my father from his rule. He would not have even suffered through a vote. I must battle him."

Warriors began talking amongst themselves while the wives at the table very slowly stood and moved to stand behind them, for protection, I assumed.

Stephanie reached for my hand. I jerked away and shook my head. "My place is by his side."

Her eyes widened before she nodded and then grabbed Genesis and Hope and moved behind the warriors, not that she of all people needed protection.

Ethan and Alex eyed Mason. It looked like they were having some sort of conversation because Alex kept laughing, and Ethan kept rolling his eyes before finally, all three of them shook hands.

The men walked off behind the warriors, leaving me and Mason with Cassius.

Cassius turned to us. "Force the truth out of him before you end his life. I have a feeling you know the exact way to make sure his soul is carried where it deserves to be carried, despite his actions here. Time makes us bitter, bitterness leads to a deep-rooted hatred, not put there by The Creator."

With those cryptic words, he moved to stand in front of the warriors.

They all seemed to breathe a sigh of relief. Nobody seemed to want to have to protect an archangel.

And fail.

"So…" His father stood. "…is this how it's going to be? I am forced to kill my son and his mate?" His grin was menacing. "Can't say it's the first time I've delighted in killing a mate."

Mason's body shook with rage.

I pressed a hand to his arm.

He sighed, and his eyes searched mine before he hung his head. "Stand by Cassius."

"But…"

I nodded and moved to take my place in front of the warriors. I didn't know what power I had. But I wasn't going to hide in back, when all I wanted to do was to stand in front and take the hit for him.

I was not meant to be still when it came to my mate.

I was not meant to watch him fight for us.

I knew it in my blood; I was made to fight beside him, fight for him. I clenched my hands.

"Patience," Cassius whispered. "Your time will come, little one."

"I'm not little."

"You choose now to fixate on your lack of height?" His lips twitched. "Such a human thing to do."

"Weren't you human for thirty days and—"

He flashed me a *"stop talking"* look.

I grinned in triumph and then looked back to Mason and nodded.

"The second time?" Mason finally said after a few seconds, his eyes flashed. "You've killed a mate before?".

His father moved around his chair and very slowly pulled his suit jacket from his massive body, folded it and placed it neatly on his chair. Then he removed his cufflinks and rolled up the sleeves of his starched white shirt.

Tarik moved toward Mason, his face indifferent until Mason's father turned his glare to Tarik and sneered. "Isn't that right, Tarik?"

Tarik froze, his face crumbling right before my eyes. "Father, not here."

"Yes, here!" His father roared, and the room seemed to shake with his fury. "Your brother's only job was to turn away the human mate and give her to you! And he played his part well. Didn't you, Tarik? Until you couldn't keep your eyes from her, until you couldn't deny your feelings for her, for your brother's wife!"

"STOP!" Tarik roared, throwing his hands against the large table. Quickly, they shifted to claws as his nails dug in. "This will change nuthin!"

"Oh?" His father laughed.

Mason stilled.

"I think it does. You see, Mason, your first mate wasn't even yours, but you were so desperate for love after your mother's death. I made a promise never to let you find your true mate. I made an oath in blood as did her parents. This was never meant to be. It was a world we could not control, one where the Watchers held too much power, the goddesses held too much power. It was the only way." A flicker of sadness seemed to flash across his face before it was gone.

"You killed her," Mason said softly, without a hint of sadness — just, maybe regret. "You not only stole her from the rightful son and gave her to me, but you lied, and then when you saw both sons fall in love with her, you killed her."

"He didn't have to," Tarik whispered.

All eyes fell to his brother.

Tarik looked away, his expression tense. "Mther killed herself to free you, Mason. Blood must always be spilled, and she knew the only way to free you of never finding your true mate was to spill her own. When Father found out, he went on a rage. He was going to kill you once and for all. Your wine was drugged. You thought she had fallen asleep next to you, but she held a dagger over your head, your own mate. I walked in before the blade cut into your skin, before Father walked in. I called in a favor." His eyes fell to Cassius.

Mason lowered his head. "Sarial."

I knew Sarial was Cassius' father, one of the original Watchers, the most powerful, an archangel of the fallen who'd spilled his own angelic blood and rejoined The Creator, but not without bestowing his wings and gifts upon his one and only son, Cassius.

Just another memory I was sure Cassius now possessed.

The room moaned and groaned with the secrets and hurt from the past.

"ENOUGH!" His father bellowed. "This changes nuthin! I am king!"

"You killed a human!" Mason roared. "That is against our laws! We protect the earth. We protect the humans!"

"Kings make hard decisions, Mason. It's what we do." He chuckled. "Hell, the first hard decision you were faced with you ran!" The room was silent. "Think you're so different now? With your goddess by your side?"

I was ready to rain fury down on him when Mason roared toward the ceiling. In a flash, he was in wolf-form.

Completely black. With red streaks down his back like his hair.

He was massive.

A wolf with muscles that shouldn't exist.

Every part of him was feral, angry.

I didn't want to be afraid.

But I was.

His father transformed just as fast.

His wolf was pitch-black with eyes of coal.

But although he was large, he wasn't near the size of Mason.

Mason was half the size of the dinner table.

His claws were larger than my head.

And he had four.

The two faced off in the middle of the floor.

Tarik didn't transform.

The room crackled with tension.

And Mason raised his claw in the air and struck first blood.

CHAPTER FORTY-ONE

MASON

I COULDN'T SEE past the rage. He had killed an innocent. The woman had not even been meant for me. I hated the sense it made. Why she often complained of me being too big, of being a brute.

A true mate would desire that.

And she hadn't craved me the way I craved her.

She'd loved me the best way she could — with half her heart — while my brother claimed the other. I knew the type of man he was; he would never have acted on his instincts, and for that, I wanted to rage.

We'd mated once.

Never to mate again.

That was the rule.

I had been given a second chance, or so I thought. What about him?

It was the first thing I would demand as king — after I killed my father. And once the thought was in my head....

The killing....

I could not help but let it fester until my body transformed into my wolf, until I felt the secrets of the Watcher inside me burst free.

Secrets of the wolves.

Where to strike. How to strike.

It was as if Gadreel's entire mind had been uploaded to mine, showing me how to defeat, how to become king.

I thanked him in that moment, wondering if I would ever get the chance to see The Creator myself — and also the Watcher he'd taken back to heaven who selfishly and then not so selfishly sacrificed his soul so that I would become what I was.

What I was born to be, however wrong it had started.

The Creator had the final say.

Power rolled through my veins. My blood soared as I struck my father's head and knocked it against the table.

The marble split in two before he stumbled forward and tried to grab my neck. I flipped him over my back and shoved him to the ground.

Killing a wolf was nearly impossible.

But I am not just a wolf. I smiled at that thought.

"You would never kill your own father. You walked away. You'll do it again." His taunting wasn't helping his case. "I sent them for her."

I pressed a claw to his throat, and his voice sounded in

my head.

"I sent them to attack her, to kill her. Did you know she's searched for you every year since your mate's death? Since the bond was broken? She would hunt for you. She would cry. It was pathetic how many times her own parents had to wipe her memories, how many times they cried over their broken-hearted daughter."

I slammed him against the ground, harder this time.

The voice in my head, my father's, kept taunting as his eyes glistened with fury. *"She was supposed to die. She is an abomination."*

I answered aloud. "You swore to protect her."

"I dinna know what I was promising. It was wrong, what they did to her, what they did to you. We will not mix with that blood!"

I smirked inwardly and struck his neck with my fangs, drawing his bitter blood and spitting it out to the side.

You were saying?

"What are you?" He pushed at me with all his force.

Wolf. Vampire. Fallen. I felt the loss of my wings so harshly I sucked in a breath. *And now? I am King.*

I struck again and slid my claws on either side of his head, making it impossible for him to move, then grabbed a piece of marble and shoved it in his heart.

He was not dead.

Not yet.

I fell to my knees and moved to my human form. Tarik tossed me a pair of jeans, and I quickly turned and put them on just in time for someone to run in the room screaming.

"Movement in the forests!"

But it was too late.

"They're here," my father said cryptically. "You did this.

This is on you." He still wasn't moving.

Hooded figures slowly entered the room and walked toward us. Twelve of them, black hair peeking out from under the hoods.

One stepped forward and pulled her hood back before looking to the right and smiling. "Daughter."

CHAPTER FORTY-TWO

SERENITY

"Danu," I whispered my mother's name. She was the one who'd given birth to me, and now I slowly walked to her outstretched arms.

She smiled and opened them wider. "I have waited centuries to finally see you."

"Why?" I choked back my tears. "Why did you wait?"

Danu looked over my head to Cassius. "I was not allowed to intervene. The Creator made it so, but when you finally found your mate I was released from that promise. It should have been centuries ago. It was, after all, promised to me."

"You know nae what ye do!" Mason's father was still

bellowing as blood spewed from his throat. "The Watchers will come! They will destroy us! They are awake!"

People grumbled around us.

I tried to hide my smile.

Mason turned to his father. "And the rightful king — the Watchers listen to him."

"It will nae matter, as long as Bannick lives!"

Danu's eyes fell to the ground as if she too believed the lie.

"Bannick is dead." Alex stepped away from the warriors. "Or at least, he's suffering and wishing he was. He was taken to the abyss." He shrugged. "You're welcome, by the way."

Mason's father sputtered, "Impossible!"

"Your fear has controlled you for too long." Mason shook his head, "Release it before I send your soul away."

"Nae!" He shook his head left and right. Blood caked his lips. "You canna do that! You dinna know how!"

Danu reached for my hand and squeezed. Then she turned to Mason and gave a single nod as she and the others stepped out of the way.

Mason outstretched his hands as dirt began circling his wrists, and then all at once, he spoke in a booming voice. "Those who watch! The king demands your presence by order of The Creator. You are summoned!"

The halls shook.

I gripped Danu's hand tighter as the sound of thunder filled the room so loudly I had to cover my ears.

And then… pitch-black.

No lights.

Until… a flicker of light.

And another.

With each flicker, one more being appeared.

Until every single one of the Watchers faced us, with their black and red hair and menacing faces.

And when I looked down at their feet…

I saw pieces of black feathers that soon turned to ash.

Danu sucked in a breath. "It has been… eons. And yet their beauty strikes me again, just as it did before. Marked by the creator, they are both holy and fallen, trapped in a purgatory of their own making. May the creator have mercy."

It was Armaros who stepped forward first, his expression stern. He stood chest to chest with Mason, their height matched, their strength equal.

Very slowly, he bent a knee and hung his head.

Every single Watcher followed.

Until they were all kneeling before the rightful ruler.

"King of the Earth. protector of humans, we ask for your blessing."

"And you will fight with us, not against us." Mason said it as a statement.

Armaros looked up and whispered, "Only if the creator will restore our song to the heavens."

Danu sucked in a breath next to me. "He has no right to ask that."

"And yet…" Armaros turned his attention to Danu. "…I am, goddess." He shook his head as a haunted expression filled his face, and then he looked to me. "For what it is worth, Serenity, I am sorry for our part in this. I am sorry that our desperation took us far enough to look the other way when our own used his power to seduce your mother, when one of our own used his own blood to create a bond between you. But our power is limitless. *His* is divine." He pointed up, "And we have been separated from it for too long to not go mad. A voice, a simple voice, a song… it is all I demand. The songs of old, so we can communicate with the heavens again, while serving our time here."

Mason held out his hand over Armaros' head as pieces of dirt fell from his hands and touched Armaros' face. A silver tear ran down Armaros' cheek before a loud ripping sound was heard.

When Armaros stood, red, black, and white wings spread wide across his back. His stunned expression said it all. And then more silver tears joined the first as he turned to see his brothers all had the same wings.

"What have you done!" Mason's father roared, throwing all his energy into getting the stake out of his body. After he removed it, he staggered to his feet to see every set of eyes on him.

"Take his soul." Mason eyed one of the Watchers who, with one nod, walked forward.

"No!" his father bellowed. "I am KING!"

CHAPTER FORTY-THREE

MASON

I FELT PITY for my father.

For the first time in my existence.

It was the only reason his soul wasn't going into the abyss where we'd sent Bannick for his evil.

"I will take him." Hanim walked forward. "The Creator will not let me see his face, but I can take him to the angels gathered at the place where souls rest."

I jerked my attention to Cassius, whose eyes had suddenly turned white, his hair glowing, and then the room was filled with the music of the heavens as angels descended one by one flanking the Watchers and every single warrior in the room.

Stunned and in utter disbelief, I watched The Creator walk forward, no longer in the image of a boy.

But a man who looked much like the Watchers and Cassius, with jet-black hair and skin of every single color, changing with each movement. Just like his eyes never fully decided on a shape — almond, circular, slanted — it was impossible to focus on his face because of the way it glowed and shifted, the way it moved to show every ethnicity ever created.

His hands, however, were outstretched.

He faced the Watchers and solidified into a normal=looking man without flaws, a man who looked like he smiled often, if the crinkles at his eyes were any indication. It was a form he took, for what purpose I had no idea. Maybe so nobody would weep in his presence or run screaming in terror.

"The songs of old are sacred," The Creator said, his voice carrying like a song across the wind. "They are also old."

Was that a joke?

Nobody laughed.

But his lips twitched as if he was amused with himself. "You all were given a choice. Bannick chose wrong, and he is suffering greatly for it. But you, being stuck in this world, stuck in a purgatory of your own making, you chose the very king I put in charge of this realm, of the earth and all its goodness. You did not choose out of selfish ambition. You chose to be reunited with me. How could I look down on my children and not see the beautiful disaster you created, only focusing on the beauty, not the mess?"

Armaros swayed like he was going to pass out.

"Ah, you are a mess." He put his hand on Armaros' shoulder. "But I would rather see a mess than perfection.

This world is not perfect. But Armaros, it is good, and you have not been forgotten. Not a day goes by I don't think of you. I think of the goodness you brought on the mountain. I think of your beauty, and I think of your dedication. Your punishment must be served, but I think it is time the ban is lifted. You have finally restored what was broken here, in this room, with the immortals without knowing it by following the very soul you were blessed with upon creation."

He stood back and then pressed a hand to Armaros' head and very slowly made his way to each Watcher, saying similar things about their talents, their character, going as far as to kiss their cheeks and hug them as if they were long-lost children who'd finally found their way home.

And maybe they were.

Stunned, I watched as The Creator turned and made his way toward me.

I wanted to back away. To run from certain judgment. I was the least perfect. I had done things. I had run from my position. I had done so many unforgivable things. And I felt my shame like a blanket choking my body.

"Mason…" The Creator inclined his head. "…it seems you've finally found your mate."

Hadn't expected that.

I nodded again.

He held out his hand to Serenity.

Slowly, she walked toward him and placed her hand in his. Danu followed after her.

"True love will always be worth it, even when you wait as long as you have," He put her hand on mine and winked. "Take care of the earth I created, the dirt beneath your feet, the animals, the humans. Take great care of the immortals." He hesitated and looked over his shoulder. "And Alex, try not to make Cassius' life so difficult every day."

Alex's jaw nearly came unhinged, and then he shrugged as if he'd think about it, but not before nodding slightly.

The creator's eyes fell to Danu. He reached for her with his free hand and tilted her chin toward him. "Do you wish to return to your realm or remain?"

Her eyes widen. "I cannot speak for my people. I speak only for myself. I wish to remain."

Someone took a step forward. "We remain with our queen."

"You will be stripped of your power if you stay," he said carefully, "But you will remain immortal."

"I accept…" Danu nodded. "…gladly."

The rest nodded their heads.

The creator finally looked down to Mason's father and shook his head. "You are lucky your son has given you mercy, I would not have been so generous." He placed a hand to his chest, and with two breaths, Mason's father died, his body lifeless.

The Creator held out his hand to Armaros. "Bring his soul."

In a flash, they were gone.

And suddenly, a song so beautiful filled the air. I could hardly breathe with the sound of it.

Every Watcher was singing in an angelic tongue that swept its way through the room with such force that a warm wind slapped against my cheek as I stared down at my mate, my life.

With a smile, she very slowly knelt in front of me, grabbed both hands, and whispered, "My king."

The entire room followed.

Including every angel, before they vanished, leaving the

room less happy than before, less holy.

But no less powerful while the song swirled around me.

"I'm not worthy," I whispered.

It was Cassius who finally said, "Those who are chosen never are. That's why he chooses them."

CHAPTER
FORTY-FOUR

SERENITY

"So..." Alex cleared his throat. "...are we still going to have dinner or—"

Hope smacked him in the chest and then pulled him in for a kiss. "Never boring with you, is it?"

"I'm hungry." His eyes lit up. "Hey, here's a thought. Feel free to say yes immediately, I'll just devour you until—"

"Stop." Ethan shook his head in disgust. "It was bad enough listening to you last night."

"Then stop listening." Alex shrugged. "I'll remember noise-canceling headphones for Christmas."

"Or you could buy your own place?" Ethan suggested.

"And part from my brother? Never." Alex winked.

Ethan looked ready to strangle anyone who dared talk to him next.

I just laughed and linked arms with Mason. "Should we eat?"

He shrugged as people gathered around the broken table and then ordered the servants to present dinner.

The Watchers stayed, and although none of them ate, they did stand around by the warriors and do what they did best. What they were born to do.

They watched.

And it felt like something had been restored in their souls as they looked on, each of them smiling. Doing exactly what they were born to do.

Observe.

CHAPTER FORTY-FIVE

SERENITY

Hours later, people were still running around, talking excitedly, telling stories, drinking wine and laughing. The Watchers hadn't moved from their spots even though Alex begged one of them to blink and tried to go all *"I'm so attractive you'll start weeping"* on him.

He did flinch.

But that was it.

Until Cassius threatened to strike him with lightning.

"Serenity..." Mason gripped my hands. "...there's something you should know. Your parents... they left you in order to help release you from the curse. They chose to die so that you could live. I didn't want you to go through the rest of your existence thinking they didn't care about you, or that they cared more about each other. My father said some things before he died. He became a very bitter man. A man full of terror is a scary thing to behold. They do things out of character, out of fear. And anything done out of fear is uncontrollable in the way it impacts those we love the most." His eyes went to Tarik briefly before coming back to me.

Tears welled, and one escaped as I stood on tiptoe and kissed Mason's parted lips, tasting wine, tasting him. "Thank you. I have you now, and even if that wasn't the truth, I'm whole. Because I have you."

He sighed like he was relieved. "And I you."

"What happens to him?" I nodded to Tarik, who was standing in the corner. His face was smiling, but his eyes weren't. He looked sad.

"I'm asking a favor" was all Mason said.

"Oh?" I looked to Cassius, who nodded slowly in our direction and then stepped out of the room. "Can he do that?"

"Cassius can do much that he won't tell us," Mason said in a distant voice. "Much that he does not want to burden us with."

I spread my hands across Mason's chest. "Just like the secrets you hold from Gadreel."

"Yes." He grabbed my hand and kissed my fingertips.

Suddenly, Cassius was back with Timber next to him, Timber looking less-than-pleased, if the state of his hair was any indication.

Timber nodded his head, gave Cassius an odd look, then nodded his head again and made his way to Tarik.

Mason smiled. "Timber is just as lonely as Tarik, though

he won't admit as much to us. He was desperate enough to seek a roommate, a human roommate."

I tried not to laugh.

Mason chuckled. "Idiot."

"He would probably end up accidentally killing the roommate and feeling so guilty he'd mope for days." I shook my head.

"Ah, but a wolf-mate..." Mason chuckled at his own joke while I hit him. "...that he can't kill."

"Unless they kill each other."

"Tarik isn't the violent type, and Timber is too..." Mason frowned and looked at Cassius. "It seems Timber is feeling useless now that everything seems solved." Mason stilled. "Oh hell."

"What?"

"I know that look."

"What look?" I glanced between Cassius and Timber.

Cassius looked angrier than I'd ever seen him.

And then one of the goddesses walked right over to Timber and offered him a glass of wine.

Cassius turned and winked at us.

"That look," Mason confirmed. "You know, for being an archangel, he does seem quite happy matchmaking, like *The Bachelor*."

It was my turn to give Mason a look. "You watch *The Bachelor*?"

He looked away and took a long sip of wine. "I have no idea what you're talking about."

"Mason."

"Blame Hope! Between that and Disney, it was the only way she'd go out of my rooms some days."

"I'm glad she did." I grabbed his hand.

"Me too."

"Now, I really am Lion King." He seemed overjoyed at this. "Or Wolf King, but it's practically the same thing."

Alex just happened to walk by and start singing the African theme song but not before Cassius snapped his fingers and lit part of Alex's leather pants on fire.

Hope dumped her wine on them and laughed.

"The world is in good hands." I smiled into my wine glass.

Mason turned his eyes to me and held my gaze. "Yes. It is."

EPILOGUE

TIMBER

The ache intensified in my chest — yet I knew my soul was present. I knew it just like I knew I was breathing. The temptation to turn toward darkness was always present, and I knew the more I isolated myself the more it would pull at me. Two different races — one good, one born for evil.

I took a staggering breath as I looked around the room.

What had possessed me to take Tarik under my wing? A wolf?

A pup?

I had books older than him!

Damnation!

I grabbed another glass of wine as the woman who'd approached me earlier locked eyes with me.

I knew exactly who she was.

She knew me.

I didn't say a word.

Or breathe it aloud.

It was forbidden.

It had been wrong.

It had also been so good.

Twice a year, I'd touch her.

Twice a year, we'd met.

And then, we'd both walked back to our separate prisons, never to breathe a word of it to anyone again.

And now, she was here.

It was wrong on so many levels I had trouble seeing straight. To mix such good with evil.

To mix at all.

And yet, when I looked around, that was all I saw, blood mixing, doing exactly what the creator had warned us against.

I had to wonder what the ramifications would be in the future for our people, for the humans. The creator never said we wouldn't suffer consequences of our actions. He simply said he'd made it for good.

I knew the creator. I knew the way his words worked.

And I knew it wasn't over. It was a battle for the ages. For the souls of every human that existed. For the souls of every race, even the immortals.

Evil never died down. It simply went into hibernation.

I glanced back at her.

She was gone.

And then I felt a hand on my back. Slowly I turned. The temptation was too great.

She licked her lips.

I looked down and gave my head a shake.

The temptation was too great. How many times had I thought of her in my dreams, clung to her scent, refusing to wash clothes because it left the air too soon?

She reached out to touch me, just as Danu called her back.

It wasn't just forbidden. It was their only sin.

To give up their virginity, especially to the leader of the demon race.

Her eyes begged me.

And I was lost again.

And I knew it was only a matter of time before I chose wrong, and my soul was damned, never to be given a second chance, all because of the one woman I could never say no to, who made me feel like I was kissing the face of heaven.

ABOUT THE
AUTHOR

Rachel Van Dyken is the New York Times, Wall Street Journal, and USA Today Bestselling author of regency and contemporary romances. When she's not writing you can find her drinking coffee at Starbucks and plotting her next book while watching The Bachelor.

She keeps her home in Idaho with her Husband, adorable son, and two snoring boxers! She loves to hear from readers!

Want to be kept up to date on new releases? Text MAFIA to 66866!

You can connect with her on Facebook or join her fan group Rachel's New Rockin Readers. And make sure to check out her website.

ALSO BY
RACHEL VAN DYKEN

Eagle Elite
Elite
Elect
Entice
Elicit
Bang Bang
Enchant
Enforce
Ember
Elude
Empire
Enrage

The Bet Series
The Bet

The Wager
The Dare

Seaside Series
Tear
Pull
Shatter
Forever
Fall
Strung
Eternal

Seaside Pictures
Capture
Keep
Steal

Waltzing With The Wallflower
Waltzing with the Wallflower
Beguiling Bridget
Taming Wilde

London Fairy Tales
Upon a Midnight Dream
Whispered Music
The Wolf's Pursuit
When Ash Falls

Renwick House
The Ugly Duckling Debutante
The Seduction of Sebastian St. James
The Redemption of Lord Rawlings
An Unlikely Alliance
The Devil Duke Takes a Bride

Ruin Series
Ruin
Toxic

Fearless
Shame

The Consequence Series
The Consequence of Loving Colton
The Consequence of Revenge
The Consequence of Seduction

The Dark Ones Series
The Dark Ones
Untouchable Darkness
Dark Surrender
Darkest Temptation

Wingmen Inc.
The Matchmaker's Playbook
The Matchmaker's Replacement

The Bachelors of Arizona
The Bachelor Auction
The Playboy Bachelor

Curious Liaisons
Cheater
Cheater's Regret

Players Game
Fraternize

Other Titles
The Parting Gift
Compromising Kessen
Savage Winter
Divine Uprising
Every Girl Does It
RIP

RACHEL VAN DYKEN BOOKS

CPSIA information can be obtained
at www.ICGtesting.com
Printed in the USA
BVOW08s1632241117
501093BV00025B/1692/P